THE DOUBLE ALIBI

Paul Halter books from Locked Room International:
The Lord of Misrule (2010)
The Fourth Door (2011)
The Seven Wonders of Crime (2011)
The Demon of Dartmoor (2012)
The Seventh Hypothesis (2012)
The Tiger's Head (2013)
The Crimson Fog (2013)
(Publisher's Weekly Top Mystery 2013 List)
The Night of the Wolf (collection, 2013)
The Invisible Circle (2014)
The Picture from the Past (2014)
The Phantom Passage (2015)
Death Invites You (2016)
The Vampire Tree (2016)
(Publisher's Weekly Top Mystery 2016 List)
The Madman's Room (2017)

Other impossible crime novels from Locked Room International:
The Riddle of Monte Verita (Jean-Paul Torok) 2012
The Killing Needle (Henry Cauvin) 2014
The Derek Smith Omnibus (Derek Smith) 2014
(Washington Post Top Fiction Books 2014)
The House That Kills (Noël Vindry) 2015
The Decagon House Murders (Yukito Ayatsuji) 2015
(Publisher's Weekly Top Mystery 2015 List)
Hard Cheese (Ulf Durling) 2015
The Moai Island Puzzle (Alice Arisugawa) 2016
(Washington Post Summer Book List 2016)
The Howling Beast (Noël Vindry) 2016
Death in the Dark (Stacey Bishop) 2017
The Ginza Ghost (Keikichi Osaka) 2017
The Realm of the Impossible (anthology) 2017
Death in the House of Rain (Szu-Yen Lin) 2017

Visit our website at www.mylri.com or
www.lockedroominternational.com

THE DOUBLE ALIBI

Le Double Alibi

Noël Vindry

Translated by John Pugmire

The Double Alibi

This book is a work of fiction. The characters, incidents, and dialogue are drawn from the author's imagination and are not to be construed as real. Any resemblance to actual events or persons, living or dead, is entirely coincidental.

First published in French in 1934 by
Librairie GALLIMARD as *Le Double Alibi*
THE DOUBLE ALIBI
English translation copyright © by John Pugmire 2018.

Every effort has been made to trace the holders of copyright. In the event of any inadvertent transgression of copyright, the editor would like to hear from the author's representatives. Contact me at pugmire1@ yahoo.com.

Cover design by Joseph Gérard

For information, contact: pugmire1@yahoo.com

FIRST AMERICAN EDITION
Library of Congress Cataloguing-in-Publication Data
Vindry, Noël
[*Le Double Alibi* English]
The Double Alibi / Noël Vindry
Translated from the French by John Pugmire

Introduction

Noël Vindry and the Puzzle Novel

Noël Vindry (1896-1954), wrote twelve locked room novels between 1932 and 1937, of a quality and quantity to rival his contemporary, John Dickson Carr (1905-1977), the American writer generally acknowledged to be the master of the sub-genre. Yet today Vindry remains largely forgotten by the French-speaking world and almost completely unknown in the English-speaking.

I first learned about Noël Vindry from Roland Lacourbe, the noted French locked room expert and anthologist, who calls him "the French John Dickson Carr." Much of what follows is taken from *Enigmatika No. 39: Noël Vindry,* a private publication edited by Jacques Baudou, Roland Lacourbe and Michel Lebrun, with a contribution from the author's son, Georges Vindry.

Noël Vindry came from an old Lyon family from whom he inherited his passion for culture and gourmet cuisine. Shortly after acquiring a Bachelor of Philosophy degree, he enlisted in the army, where he fought with distinction, earning a *Croix de Guerre,* but was invalided out in 1915 with severe lung damage.

During his long convalescence he studied and mastered law sufficiently to become a deputy *juge d'instruction* (examining magistrate)—a position unique to countries practising the Napoleonic Code, under which a single jurist is given total authority over a case, from investigating crime scenes to questioning witnesses; from ordering the arrest of suspects to preparing the prosecution's case, if any (see Appendix 1.)

He was appointed to serve in Aix-en-Provence in the south of France which, at the time, boasted the second largest Appeals Court outside of Paris, and which he chose because of its climate. Known as the "city of a thousand fountains," it holds a music festival every year to rival those of Bayreuth, Glyndebourne and Salzburg. In Vindry's time, it was known as *La Belle Dormante (Sleeping Beauty)* because

5

"at night you can hear the grass growing in the streets," according to Georges Vindry.

His first novel, *La Maison Qui Tue (The House That Kills),* appeared in 1932, the same year as Carr's fourth, *The Waxworks Murder.* Both books featured detectives who were *juges d'instruction:* Vindry's M. Allou and Carr's Henri Bencolin. Vindry's narrator, Lugrin, is the same age as his creator when he entered chambers, but there are few other autobiographical touches.

Vindry's book and the others that swiftly followed attracted considerable interest and, by the mid-1930s, he was one of the three most successful mystery writers in the French-speaking world, along with the two Belgian authors Georges Simenon and Stanislas-Andre Steeman. He is the only one of the three not to have had any of his books translated into English, until LRI's *The House That Kills* (2015), or brought to the screen.

In France, Vindry was hailed as the undisputed master of the "puzzle novel *(roman probleme*),"* a term he himself coined. In an essay on the detective novel written in 1933, he distinguished between the adventure novel**; the police novel; and the puzzle novel. The first deals with the acts of the criminal; the second with the capture of the criminal; and the third with the unmasking of the criminal. He held that the puzzle novel should be constructed like a mathematical problem: at a certain point, which is emphasised, all the clues will have been provided fairly, and the rigorous solution will become evident to the astute reader.

Allou himself is a deliberately dry figure about whom we learn very little. The plot and the puzzle are everything. Descriptive passages, even of entire countrysides, are kept to a minimum, as are any revelations in the narrative about characters' feelings: the omnipresent dialogue allows people to define themselves, providing ample opportunity for deception.

Already by 1934 there were rumblings from French critics that the puzzle novel, as so consummately practiced by Noël Vindry, failed to give full rein to character development.

*I prefer "puzzle novel" to "problem novel" which I feel is too ambiguous

**the detective/criminal adventure in the manner of Edgar Wallace's *The Four Just Men* and 174 other novels.

In vain had Vindry pointed out in his essay the previous year that: "The detective novel, as opposed to the psychological one, does not see the interior but only the exterior. 'States of mind' are prohibited, because the culprit must remain hidden." Nevertheless, the prominent critic Robert Brasillach asserted in *Marianne* (April, 1934) that the reign of the puzzle novel was already over and there were no more tricks left with which to bamboozle the jaded reader! (For the record, this was before Carr's *The Hollow Man* in 1935; Carter Dickson's *The Judas Window* and Clayton Rawson's *Death from a Top Hat* in 1938; and Pierre Boileau's *Six Crimes Sans Assassin*, with its six impossible murders, in 1939.) It was time to embrace crime novels rich in characterisation and atmosphere —such as those written by one M. Georges Simenon, for example.

Simenon, as is well-known, disdained the puzzle novel (despite having written several good puzzle short stories in his early career as Georges Sim) because he saw it as too rigid and too much under the influence of Anglo-Saxon writers. In his novels, the plot and the puzzle—if there is one—are a distant second to atmosphere and the psychology of the characters: the complete antithesis of Vindry's works. And, to further distance himself from the classical detective fiction of the period, it is the humble policeman and not the gifted amateur or the high functionary who solves the case. Thus were the seeds of the police procedural planted at the very peak of the Golden Age.

From 1932 to 1937 both Simenon and Vindry wrote at the same frantic rate as John Dickson Carr/Carter Dickson. After that, Vindry wrote only one more puzzle novel before World War II. Even though he announced on a Radio Francaise broadcast in 1941 that he was abandoning detective fiction because it didn't amuse him any more, he nevertheless wrote three more shortly before he died in 1954; none of them featured M. Allou and, after such a long break from his earlier success, his books failed to sell well.

By this time, however, his views had mellowed and he had become more accommodating towards the detective novel, which he defined, in a 1953 letter to the editor of *Mystère-Magazine* (see Appendix 2), as "a mystery drama emphasizing logic," and consisting of three elements:

1. A drama, the part with the action
2. A mystery, the poetic part
3. The logic, the intelligent part

"They are terribly difficult to keep in equilibrium. If drama dominates, we fall into melodrama or worse, as everyone knows; if mystery dominates, we finish up with a fairy tale, something altogether different which doesn't obey the same laws of credibility; if logic dominates, the work degenerates into a game, a chess problem or a crossword and it's no longer a novel."

A great example of equilibrium? Gaston Leroux's *Le Mystere de la Chambre Jaune (The Mystery of the Yellow Room)* published in 1908. This, of course, was also declared by Carr to be the greatest locked room mystery of all.

Meanwhile, Simenon powered on and was next rivalled by Boileau- Narcejac. Pierre Boileau and Thomas Narcejac, individually successful as puzzle novel writers, teamed up following an award dinner for Narcejac to which Boileau, as a previous winner, had been invited. Their novels, while maintaining the brilliant puzzle plots dreamt up by Boileau, relaxed the rigid puzzle novel formula espoused by Vindry and incorporated Narcejac's descriptive and character work.

Although he may have been a shooting star, Noël Vindry was much admired by his peers. Steeman, in a letter to Albert Pigasse, the founder of *Le Masque,* in 1953, suggested that, even though Vindry's latest work was his weakest, he deserved a prize which everyone— readers and critics alike—would realise was for the ensemble of his work. Narcejac, writing in *Combat* after Vindry's death in 1954, asserted that nobody, not even "those specialists E. Queen and D. Carr" *(sic),* was the equal of the master, Noël Vindry. Even though the puzzle-novel was well and truly dead, if he had to designate its poet, he would not hesitate: it would be Vindry. And, in their 1964 memoir on *Le Roman Policier* (The Detective Novel), Boileau and Narcejac spoke of his "unequalled virtuosity" and "stupefying puzzles."

If Golden Age Detection needed a patron saint, then Noël Vindry would surely be a candidate.   JMP

Chapter I

ANXIETY

In the village, they were known as "the Misses Levalois," without distinguishing one from the other, because no one had ever dealt with either of them apart from the other. They went out together; walked with the same tiny steps; had the same grey hair, the same wrinkles, the same expressionless eyes—how could they recognise their own hats and coats? They must pick them at random.

And so it was that, little by little, Hortense and Gertrude became a single being with two heads, "the Misses Levalois."

They were well enough thought of in the village because they possessed just the right degree of affluence to command respect without provoking jealousy. Their house, somewhat isolated at one end of the high street, was small but in good condition and scrupulously well maintained. Far from being spendthrifts, they weren't tight-fisted either. Whilst they would never have given money to the poor—after all, they didn't know them—they always put a little money aside for the church collection.

Four times a year they took the tram to Lyon and returned with their arms full of small packages. These trips constituted the only events in their lives in the sixty years of their existence in the village.

Well, not quite. There was one other: ten years ago they had taken in a penniless older aunt.

Although old, Aunt Dorothée wasn't that much older than her nieces. She was only ten years their elder, but years of hard work had aged her prematurely.

She was already bent over and walking with a cane when "the Misses Levalois" had brought her back with them from Lyon. Since then, her head had sagged further and she had needed a second cane. Even so, she held herself well in the circumstances and hobbled to church every morning, whatever the weather.

The sisters were highly thought of for that act of charity, particularly since no extravagance ensued: Aunt Dorothée was destitute, although she might inherit a modest fortune one day. Her

9

brother, an old miser living in Lyon, seemed certain to leave her something eventually, so the generosity of her nieces was within reasonable limits, and the peasants of Limonest respected them all the more for it.

***

That evening, the sisters prepared dinner as usual. But, since it was a Thursday, they added a fourth place setting. Three times a week, there was a guest—always the same one, naturally.

On each such occasion, either Gertrude or Hortense would unfailingly announce, in a loud voice:

'We'll bring out the best silverware.'

It was a compliment addressed to their aunt, who had been left twelve place settings in ornamental silver, and who had sworn never to sell them, even in the worst of times. Her husband, a drunkard, had sold everything else, down to the furniture, but she had hidden them from him until his death. They were a reminder of the times when she had lived comfortably with her parents, and over time she had come to attach an inestimable value to them. They were a guarantee of her dignity, and, from time to time, she would open the sideboard drawer to look lovingly at them.

That was why her nieces never failed to use them on those evenings when their "lawyer" came to dinner.

But he hadn't been a lawyer in Limonest.

The title had been conferred in good faith on Mr. Epicevieille, Esquire, because he hinted at it in each conversation:

'When I was leading that important study, one of the first in Lyon....'

People concluded he must have been a lawyer. In fact, he'd never been more than a second clerk.

But his physical appearance, even more than his words, helped with the illusion. Tall, thin, and dry, he held himself very straight, despite his advanced years, and was never seen wearing anything but a frock coat with an overlarge collar and a white tie.

It should have aroused curiosity that a noted lawyer from Lyon should choose to retire to Limonest in a tiny apartment, without even a housekeeper, and preparing his own meals—which must have been frugal, according to the village grocer. But his words were so ponderous and weighty, and his appearance so stern, that people forgot everything else and Epicevieille had become "the lawyer" to everyone.

Needless to say, upon his arrival five years ago, he'd made a point of visiting the notables of the village. He'd made a good impression everywhere, but nowhere more so than with the Misses Levalois. He'd given them some financial advice, which had been very sound, since when they'd considered him someone of importance, which is why they invited him three times a week.

That night, as usual, he arrived punctually, just as the church bells began to strike seven o'clock.

Each time they would sit down to eat, Hortense and Gertrude would take turns to serve. The dishes were copious and, each time one appeared, the "lawyer" would unfailingly announce with compunction:

'You're tempting me. I really shouldn't....'

He would give the impression, just as he had with the grocer, that it was on doctor's orders that he ate so little. But, as their guest, he would readily devour half a chicken.

'Your cooking is so tempting,' he would explain.

'Good food never hurt anyone,' Hortense or Gertrude—and sometimes both together—would reply.

It was the same that evening. Once the meal was over, Epicevieille prepared to digest it peacefully in the huge, soft armchair reserved for him.

But, to his great annoyance, he heard the request he dreaded the most:

'Please explain to our aunt, *maître,* what to think of her nephew Gustave.'

Hardly a month went by without them making the same request. The "lawyer" let out a sigh, wiped the anticipatory beatific smile off his face, replaced it with a stern, majestic look, and began in a solemn voice:

'It's certain, madam, that he's not someone to be recommended.'

The circumlocution, severe though it appeared, was an understatement. In fact, Gustave Allevaire deserved to be called a criminal.

Not that he'd committed a really serious crime yet. His offences were less serious but numerous, including petty theft, breach of trust, and swindling. At forty years of age, he'd racked up eight convictions, of which three had warranted more than three months in prison.

The number was crucial, for another offence would result in him being sent to Guyane, a prison for habitual offenders; and should the sentence be for three months or more, it would be hard labour for him.

Such behaviour, as can be imagined, had driven the respectable old maids to despair. Gustave Allevaire was their first cousin. Just as hard to accept as his disdain for moral laws was the shame he'd brought on the family.

At the beginning, they'd put on a brave face and housed the miscreant during his periods of misery. Then, as they became fearful that people in the village would start to recognise his name and family ties and learn of his misadventures, their welcome became more reserved: the risk of shame outweighed the pleasure they felt when lecturing him and setting him an example.

They had in fact, before their Aunt Dorothée had come to stay, decided not to invite him any more. But their resolve withered in the face of the old woman's stubbornness.

That stubbornness was comparable only to the forces of nature: powerful, blind and obstinate. Old Aunt Dorothée could only imagine her nephew as he had been when she was bringing him up. For her, he had never grown up, and therefore had never changed.

For the last fifteen years, her bad sight had prevented her from reading a newspaper, so her knowledge of the world was limited by what people told her. When it came to Gustave, she would shake her head whilst listening to his cousins, all the while insisting:

'Those are all lies. How can you imagine that little boy, with his big blue eyes, could have done such things? He's been unjustly blamed.'

In vain did Hortense and Gertrude try to explain to her that the "little boy" was now a vicious thug. Dorothée refused to change her mind. And she threatened to return permanently to her attic room if they refused to let her see her nephew.

There was scarcely a year that he failed to pay them a visit, usually just after he'd come out of prison. He claimed he was doing it to "pass a week with his family."

To be fair, his presence was not in itself disagreeable. Allevaire showed himself to be gentle and even obliging, listening to lectures with a resigned air, and lavishing his aunt with charming attention.

12

But the neighbours always showed too much interest at the smiling, elegantly dressed man, who spoke little and whose name was unknown to them.

'Is he one of your relatives?' they would ask.

'Very distant, very distant,' the sisters would reply. 'He's in business....'

And each time Allevaire left, they would chastise their aunt.

'We've had a narrow escape... Everyone is questioning us... They can't understand our silence... He's a scoundrel. One of these days something bad is going to happen here.'

'Oh, the poor dear,' Dorothée would moan.

It had been the same for the last ten years.

Since Epicevieille's arrival on the scene, the sisters had tried to use his authority to overcome the old woman's stubbornness. But his prestige paled in comparison to her memories. Hortense and Gertrude persisted nonetheless, and, for the last five years the ritual had been repeated almost every month:

'Please explain to our aunt, *maître*, what to think of her nephew Gustave.'

And each time, after a deep sigh, the "notary" would reply:

'It's certain, madam, that he's not someone to be recommended.'

He would add a few comments, in phrases which he recited automatically, always in the same form, while his mind was elsewhere.

That evening, however, there was a variation. After running through the list of offences once again, Epicevieille added, in the same solemn, slow voice:

'As a matter of fact, I'm surprised not to see him here. He's in the neighbourhood.'

'In Limonest?' exclaimed the old maids in unison.

'Not exactly, but only a few kilometres away. I saw him from a distance this afternoon, in Champagne-au-Mont-d'Or, whilst I was taking my daily walk.'

'And he didn't come to see me!' moaned Dorothée.

Her words provoked a violent reaction: Hortense and Gertrude, shedding their customary reserve, cried out at the same time:

'Well, far be it from us to regret it... He must have come to realise that his visits weren't welcome... Fortunately, we were so blunt last time that he must have realised we were showing him the door....'

'The poor dear. Where's he going to sleep?' said the old woman.

'I don't know, madam,' replied Epicevieille. 'I didn't speak to him, and I don't think he even saw me.'

'*Maître*, I beg you not to tell anyone we're related,' implored Hortense.

'Miss Hortense, please,' protested the "lawyer" with dignity. 'I'm used to keeping professional secrets.'

Ten o'clock chimed; he stood up precisely on the last strike and majestically took his leave.

The two sisters went into the kitchen to wash the dishes.

'I don't like this neighbourhood,' said Hortense. 'Gustave knows our house only too well. It would be easy for him to play a dirty trick on us.'

'Come now!' declared Gertrude. 'He'd never steal from here, where his aunt's living. He may be a scoundrel, but he genuinely loves her.'

'You're too lenient, my poor Gertrude. That kind of individual has no feelings. Think of the Libots and their son....'

And they turned to other gossip.

Chapter II

STRANGE NEWS

At one o'clock in the morning, Hortense stealthily opened the door communicating with her sister's bedroom. She tiptoed over to the bed and whispered:

'Gertrude....'

The other opened her eyes and was about to ask questions in a loud voice, but Hortense added:

'Shush ... Listen....'

Despite their age, they both had good hearing. In the silence of the night they could hear footsteps on the floor below.

'Maybe it's Aunt Dorothée,' murmured Gertrude.

'Maybe... let's look in her room.'

The aunt's room also communicated with the others. Silently, the two old maids entered and approached the bed; their aunt was lying there.

They touched her shoulder and she sat up quickly:

'What's happening?'

'Shush... Listen....'

The old woman kept quiet for a few moments, then, clutching the hands of her nieces, pronounced in an anxious voice:

'The floor downstairs is creaking... but sometimes furniture, in the night....'

'Put the thought out of your mind, aunt. Not with that kind of continuity. There's someone in the house....'

'We're lost!' moaned Gertrude.

'Not at all,' replied her sister, firmly. 'All our doors to the corridor are locked.'

'He managed to open the front door!'

'Didn't you lock it from the inside?' asked Dorothée.

'I think so.'

'I think I locked it as well.'

'What?' retorted Dorothée in astonishment. 'You can't both have locked it.'

15

'I can't remember,' admitted Gertrude. 'Sometimes it's my sister, sometimes it's me.'

'You each count on the other to do it, so it stays open! Good grief, what next? ... Ah!'

The last utterance came after a new, more metallic, noise was heard.

'They're stealing my silverware,' moaned Dorothée.

Hortense was the bravest of the three women. The others instinctively hung on to her, as if she could protect them. But all she did was to tell them not to raise their voices: the miscreant, if surprised, could kill them all!

The warning did not at all have the intended effect. A growing fear had been gripping Gertrude, the most nervous of the three, to the point that she was unable to utter a sound. But, at the thought of murder, she made a supreme effort, as if to rid herself of a gag, and released a loud cry!

After which the other two started to shout for help at the tops of their voices.

They stopped immediately they heard the sound of the door below slamming shut.

'He's run off,' announced Dorothée.

'He's run off,' repeated the two sisters.

'We've had a narrow escape!' continued Hortense. 'With all the windows and shutters closed, nobody would have heard us.'

'Nobody,' echoed Gertrude.

'But has he really gone?' asked Dorothée.

'So it seems.'

They listened for a long time in silence. No, there wasn't the slightest noise in the house. The man must really have fled.

'Suppose we take a look...' suggested Hortense after a while.

But as soon as she spoke, the two others tightened their grip on her.

'No! No! Don't go... you never know.'

Only at daybreak did they decide to go downstairs.

***

The disaster was immediately apparent. The sideboard drawer was open and Aunt Dorothée's silverware had disappeared.

'He took it! He took it!' she moaned.

Her nieces barely had time to hold her up and place a chair under her. She collapsed and hid her face in her hands. All they could hear, obstinately repeated, were the words:

'My silver place settings! My silver place settings!'

'My God!' exclaimed Gertrude. 'He also broke into the desk... Our five thousand francs!'

Hortense had already gone over to the desk and searched one of the drawers.

'Yes,' she said, 'he's taken them as well... Luckily I took the precaution not to put everything there.'

The largest part of their savings was in fact in Hortense's room, in the traditional hiding place of old maids: under the mattress.

'And it's a bit of luck,' added Gertrude, 'that there was at least some money here; the burglar must have thought it was all of our savings, so he didn't look elsewhere; otherwise he would have come upstairs to our rooms.'

The thought was enough for the two sisters to make the sign of the cross.

As for Dorothée, she wasn't listening, but just kept repeating, over and over again:

'My silver settings! My silver settings!'

That misfortune seemed to be the only thing to upset her.

Suddenly Gertrude cried out:

'My aunt! He didn't take everything!'

It was a feeble consolation, and only Gertrude's naïvety caused her to sound a triumphal note. Two spoons had, in fact, not been taken.

They were lying on the floor next to one of the chairs. It seemed that the burglar, having assembled his loot in order to place it in a sack, had been disturbed by the women's cries and, in his haste, had swept the two items to the floor and left them behind.

Dorothée was already on her feet and, with the aid of her canes, was heading towards what was left of her treasure. But Hortense stopped her in her tracks:

'Don't touch them, Aunt.'

'Why?'

'The police have to examine them. There may be... what do you call them, Gertrude? You know, the newspapers sometimes talk about them....'

'Fingerprints?'

'Yes, that's it. We mustn't touch anything here. As soon as it's daylight, I'll go and alert the gendarmes.'

Dorothée went back to sit down and immediately started to cry again.

'Perhaps you were right,' whispered Gertrude in her sister's ear.

She was only half convinced. No matter how bad her opinion of her cousin, she balked at believing he would steal the things most precious to his aunt, after she'd been so good to him.

But Hortense replied tersely:

'There are no milestones on the road to evil, Gertrude.'

Her sister recognised a sentence from a sermon somewhere and respectfully refrained from replying.

***

The gendarme sergeant, alerted by Hortense, had arrived.

'So a man supposedly got into the house clandestinely?'

His Corsican accent stressed the word, and Gertrude replied reflexively:

'Clandestinely, yes.'

'And how did he get in?'

'Through the door.'

'Obviously! He didn't go through the walls! Don't you lock the door at night?'

The two sisters looked at each other.

'Usually,' murmured Hortense, 'it's Gertrude.'

'Usually,' murmured Gertrude at the same time, 'it's Hortense.'

'You should listen to yourselves!' exclaimed the sergeant. 'Who normally locks it?'

'Both of us,' said Gertrude, in a conciliatory manner.

'Heaven help me! This investigation is not going to be a piece of cake.'

The sergeant was starting to get irritated.

'Let's start with you, miss.' He addressed himself to Gertrude. 'Did you or did you not lock the door last night?'

'I think so....'

'And you, miss?'

'I think so as well....'

'Now I think about it,' added Gertrude, intimidated by the sergeant's rising anger, 'I might have been confusing last night with the night before... All our nights are the same....'

18

'Let's drop the subject,' said the sergeant, shrugging his shoulders. 'Did the man leave any traces of his visit?'

'Two spoons,' moaned Dorothée. 'Two of my spoons. Look how beautiful they were!'

'I told everyone not to touch,' said Hortense. 'Did I do the right thing?'

'Absolutely, miss. There might be fingerprints on them.'

He picked them up carefully with his large hands and inspected them, one after the other, at an angle to the light.

'Heavens above! It's magnificent! There's a print perfectly placed next to the initials. There's not a moment to lose! I'll go to Lyon myself to alert the prosecutor's office, who will no doubt order me to deliver this spoon to the detective squad. They have anthropometric files on all the criminals in the region. It'll be child's play to identify him.'

***

'Yes, child's play,' repeated the inspector of the *police mobile*, to whom the examining magistrate had delegated the matter. 'The *Sûreté* alerted us immediately. The burglar is an old hand, we'll catch him easily.'

He was in the Levalois sisters' house when he spoke the words, and the three women listened respectfully.

'What's his name?' asked Dorothée eventually, in a feeble voice.

'Gustave Allevaire.'

The old woman fell down in a dead faint without even so much as a cry, as if someone had knocked her out.

Whilst the two nieces fussed over her, sprinkling water on her face and giving her vinegar to inhale, the inspector stood there with a frown on his face.

When Dorothée had been revived, he asked firmly:

'So, do you know him?'

'No…' said Hortense.

But, at the same time, Gertrude gave an affirmative nod.

'So now, speak! Who is he?'

Now they had to confess everything. Gertrude started to cry.

'We don't want anyone in Limonest to know we're related, inspector,' she moaned.

'It won't be me who tells them. So, is he a frequent guest?'

'Oh, no. He hasn't been here for three months.'

'Explain yourself better,' said Hortense. 'You'll make it sound as if he comes every three months. No, inspector, he didn't even come once a year. And he wasn't welcome when he did.'

'Calm down, miss, I'm not accusing you of anything. I'm just trying to understand, that's all. I wanted to know if he'd been able to get a key.'

'Well, yes. We lent him one whenever he came to stay. All he had to do was copy it.'

'And,' continued the inspector, 'is it also possible that he noticed that you shared the responsibility for locking the door, and that it was often left open?'

'Oh, I don't think so,' exclaimed the two sisters simultaneously. 'You lock it properly, don't you Gertrude?' 'You lock it properly, don't you Hortense?'

The two questions came out at the same time and the inspector was enlightened.

'So it's a very simple matter,' declared the inspector.

That's a word which should never be uttered, for it supposedly brings bad luck. It had scarcely crossed his lips when a gendarme appeared in the doorway.

'I have some very sad news for you, Madam Dorothée. Your nephew was murdered in Marseille last night.'

Chapter III

THE SCREAM IN THE NIGHT

During that night of May 9th to 10th, the Levalois residence was not the only place where people were in fear.

Three hundred kilometres away, in the small town of Aubagne, near Marseille, lived Father Grégoire. Although he didn't actually live in the town, his farm being located in open country just beyond the outskirts.

Old Father Grégoire would have lived there perfectly happily on his fertile land, if not for the problem of his pigsty. It wasn't the actual work involved which caused him concern, onerous though that was. Raising sows is far more difficult than townsfolk imagine. If the litters of piglets are not to be lost, the mother herself must be isolated, to avoid her crushing them. So they are placed in a fenced-off area, from which they are removed every four hours in order to feed at the udder. That requires getting up at night.

Father Grégoire had been doing that for fifty years and it had become so much of a habit that he scarcely noticed it. He even accepted the inconvenience of having the pigsty a hundred metres from the farmhouse itself. All that would have been nothing, were it not for the proximity of the "Black House."

It was a large building some two hundred metres from the farm, and it was shrouded in a superstitious dread. The fear was not simply due to the dark walls which had earned the house its name. The legend was very old; it was said that a horrible crime had been committed there: a man had murdered his parents. Since then it had become cursed and nobody lived there.

And yet—and this was the worst part—it wasn't completely unoccupied. On certain nights, it was said, a glimmer of light could be seen through the slits of the shutters.

Pure imagination, said the sceptics; or the reflection of the moon on the windows.

But Father Grégoire knew it to be true. He'd seen the lights from time to time, as he'd gone to take care of his pigs on very dark nights.

He readily accepted the views of those whom others ridiculed: the spirits of the dead did return sometimes.

So it was that the trip from the farmhouse to the pigsty became unbearable, particularly on those dark occasions. Which was the case on that night of May 9th to10th.

He'd gone out at around one o'clock, without a lantern because he knew the route by heart. It was at that same moment that, three hundred kilometres away, near Lyon, the three old women were huddled together in Dorothée's room.

Father Grégoire shot anxious looks in the direction of the "Black House," whose silhouette was dimly visible at the top of a hill hundreds of metres away.

Suddenly he shivered. There was a light behind one of the shutters. There was no doubt about it. Although it wasn't strong, it wasn't an optical illusion. The "spirits" had returned.

He crossed himself and started back on his route, but stopped, completely paralysed with fright: a blood-curling scream had come from the "Black House"—the scream of a man being murdered.

It was followed by total silence.

Father Grégoire dropped limply to the ground, where he stayed motionless, his heart pounding. But his fear intensified when he heard someone walking in his direction: someone coming down the hill.

With a sudden burst of energy, he dragged himself to a nearby bush to hide himself. A man walking rapidly passed by three metres away and Father Grégoire could see him perfectly. He felt slightly reassured: it wasn't a ghost.

Nevertheless, he stayed there for another half an hour, motionless. Then, not having heard any suspicious noises, he stood up and, after a brief hesitation, looked in the direction of the "Black House." He could make out its sinister silhouette; there were no lights on.

Father Grégoire proceeded to his pigsty.

When he got back to bed, he couldn't sleep. As soon as it was dawn, he went to alert the gendarmerie.

***

The sergeant was a Parisian and not very receptive to peasant legends. Since his arrival in the region three months ago, he'd heard talk of the "Black House," but hadn't paid it much attention.

His questions to Father Grégoire went straight to the point.

'So, as I understand it, the building was uninhabited?'

'There was no living person in there,' replied the farmer, carefully.

'Yes, I know. They say that sometimes there's a light in there.'

'I've seen it often with my own eyes.'

'We're going to look into all that.'

He left with one of his men; Father Grégoire walked along with them but dropped back when they got closer to the house.

The gendarmes arrived at the front door. It was only on the latch, so they went in.

The first two rooms were completely empty. It did seem as though the building was unoccupied.

But, as soon as they reached the threshold of the third room, they could see the outline of something lying on the floor. They opened the shutters: it was indeed a dead body lying there.

At the same time, they noted that there were several pieces of furniture in the room: three chairs, a bench and a table, on which stood an oil lamp.

They approached the corpse. It was that of a forty-year-old man, formally attired. There was a bloodstain on his jacket.

They unbuttoned the waistcoat and shirt and saw the wound, right in the heart; a stab wound, no doubt. But they couldn't find the actual murder weapon.

They looked at the contorted face.

'Do you know this individual?' asked the sergeant.

The gendarme, who'd lived in Aubagne for several years, swore he'd never seen the man before.

They sent for Father Grégoire, who had stopped fifty metres away, and with great difficulty persuaded him to enter the house.

'That's not someone from around here,' he declared.

They were ready to believe him, for he'd been born in Aubagne sixty years ago and had never left the town.

'Let's look in his pockets,' said the sergeant.

He pulled out several objects, notably a revolver and a wallet.

The latter contained a small amount of money and some papers: several letters—some very old and some quite recent—addressed to "M. Gustave Allevaire" and signed "Your devoted Aunt Dorothée." The address on all the envelopes was the same: "Poste Restante, Bordeaux."

Several other documents: bills, etc., confirmed that the deceased

23

was indeed Gustave Allevaire.

'I seem to remember hearing the name,' said the sergeant.

But his memory was vague and he didn't pursue the matter.

'We should notify his family and the public prosecutor,' he added.

'Whose family?' asked the gendarme.

'The aunt's, for heaven's sake! The letters are stamped Limonest: from the handwriting, she seems to be an old woman. There can't be all that many old women in Limonest with the Christian name Dorothée.'

After having taken down Father Grégoire's deposition and notified the Marseille public prosecutor by telephone, he went to the nearby post office to send a telegram to his colleague in Limonest:

'Notify old woman, first name Dorothée, that her nephew Gustave Allevaire was murdered tonight at Aubagne, near Marseille. Ask her to come urgently to identify the body.'

***

That was the telegram the gendarme was holding when he entered the Levalois residence.

The inspector snatched it from his hand and read it three times to make sure.

'It's not possible,' he growled eventually.

He turned to Dorothée, who was crying in a corner.

'Don't worry, granny, it must be a mistake,' he said. 'Your nephew wasn't in Marseille last night.'

There was no reply.

'You have to go,' he continued. 'They need you to identify the body.'

This time the old woman looked up.

'Leave for Marseille…,' she murmured, horrified.

'There must be someone who could accompany you.'

'We could go…,' murmured Hortense.

'Oh! Such a long way…,' moaned her sister.

'A long way?' exclaimed the inspector. 'It's barely three hundred kilometres.'

'It's fifty years since we took a train, Inspector.'

Just at that moment, a thin old man with erect bearing entered the room.

'Ah, *maître*,' implored Gertrude, 'please help us.'

24

'What's happened?' asked Epicevieille in his solemn voice.

'They want us to go to Marseille. Our cousin was just murdered there last night!'

'And it was he who stole Aunt Dorothée's silver,' added Hortense.

'That seems to be a contradiction,' observed Epicevieille, solemnly.

'It does, doesn't it?' said the inspector sarcastically. 'Now you understand why the family's presence is required there.'

'Yes, I understand. You have to go there, ladies.'

'Please come with us,' begged Gertrude.

'Willingly, but it's at very short notice.'

'There's a train at twelve o'clock,' intervened the inspector. 'And it's already eleven.'

'So it's quite urgent,' continued Epicevieille, 'and I wasn't prepared. I'll have to arrange a telegraphic transfer—.'

'We'll pay for everything!' exclaimed Hortense. 'It's already very kind on your part to accompany us.'

'In that case, I accept.'

The inspector turned to the gendarme:

'Find a car to transport four people to the Perrache train station.'

He thought for a moment, then added:

'In fact, I'll come with you as well. I need to discuss the case with my Marseille colleagues… It's looking very strange.'

One hour later, Dorothée, her two nieces, Epicevieille and the inspector were on their way to Marseille.

They arrived in the late afternoon. A taxi took them to the Aubagne gendarmerie.

'The magistrates are up in the house,' explained one of the gendarmes. 'I'll drive you as far as the car can go. You'll have to climb the remaining five hundred metres on foot.'

'I'll do it,' declared Dorothée firmly.

26

Chapter IV

A STUNNING TURN OF EVENTS

There were indeed two magistrates already at the "Black House": a deputy public prosecutor from Marseille and an examining magistrate.

The latter, judging from the respect accorded him by the gendarmes, had to be someone of importance. There was something more than deference in their attitude: it seemed more like admiration, which was surprising in view of the modest demeanour of the person in question.

The magistrate was M. Allou, whose perspicacity and courage provoked, at the same time, extraordinary esteem from his subordinates and suspicion amongst high-ranking court officials for his independent character, so unlike the typically neutral civil servant.

The gendarme sergeant asked him a question, in the manner of someone who expected M. Allou to be able to solve any problem at first sight.

'In your opinion, *monsieur le juge*, what was the victim doing here and who killed him?'

'I have absolutely no idea. We don't even know who owns the house!'

It had been impossible to find out. There had been no recorded changes in the land registry for over a hundred years; the government had neglected to take possession of the worthless property; and no peasant would have dared to move in.

M. Allou had not been able to make any observations beyond the obvious. A meticulous search of the building had revealed nothing. The only furniture was in the room where the crime had been committed, where three chairs, a bench and a half-empty oil lamp had been found.

The room must have been visited several times: there were ashes in the hearth and several cigarette butts of different vintages had been found on the floor.

It was quite understandable that the mysterious visitors had never

27

been seen. The building itself was perched atop an arid hill bereft of human activity. Father Grégoire's farm was the only other building in the vicinity.

Hence no discovery had been made concerning the circumstances of the crime. The medical examiner confirmed what the peasant had said: the murder had taken place between midnight and two o'clock in the morning. The man had succumbed almost immediately to the wound, and he must have been caught by surprise, because there were no traces of resistance to the struggle on the victim's body.

One could also assume that robbery had not been the motive of the crime, because several hundred francs had been found in the wallet.

'Yes,' said M. Allou, 'it bears all the marks of an act of vengeance. In any case, the man must have been taken by surprise, because you found his revolver in a buttoned-down trouser pocket.'

'That's correct, *monsieur le juge.*'

'We don't know anything more for the moment. We have to wait for the family to brief us about the kind of life this individual led and his relationships. But it could well be that the murder was so simple there's nothing to base an investigation on.'

'Oh, *monsieur le juge*, you've solved many complex cases in the past.'

'But that's much easier, sergeant. You know my method: formulate a hypothesis which accounts for all the details and then verify it by experiment. But when there aren't any strange facts, one can postulate a thousand plausible theories which are impossible to prove. I can contribute little to a banal crime such as this. I would much prefer it to be rife with contradictions!'

M. Allou was about to get his wish granted beyond his wildest dreams.

Just as he had left the building and was filling his pipe, he saw half a dozen people coming up the hill.

At the front was a gendarme. Two elderly women of identical appearance followed him, and between them was a tall, thin individual wearing a frock coat. Finally, a hundred metres behind, a very old woman struggled painfully to advance with the aid of two canes; a man was by her side ready to help her: the inspector from Lyon.

'The family,' announced the gendarme as he arrived.

M. Allou greeted the Misses Levalois, and Epicevieille bowed,

28

bending his tall form almost in half.

'Are you close relatives of the victim?' asked the magistrate.

'Yes,' replied Hortense. 'This gentleman, who is a lawyer, wished to accompany us, even though he's a stranger.' Epicevieille bowed again. 'We were first cousins.'

'Did you know your relative well?'

'Oh, yes! He came to see us almost every year.'

'Well, then, come in and see if you recognise him. It's a painful sight, but I'm obliged to inflict it on you.'

He preceded them into the room.

At the sight of the body, Gertrude let out a cry and, supporting herself with the door frame, closed her eyes. Hortense, less sensitive, advanced determinedly and looked at the body.

Then she turned towards M. Allou with a surprised look:

'But that's not Gustave!' she exclaimed.

'Are you sure?'

'Certain. It looks like him, but it isn't.'

Hearing those words, Gertrude approached. An unknown dead man frightened her less.

'No, that's not Gustave,' she agreed.

'That's not M. Allevaire,' added Epicevieille in his cavernous voice.

'Did you know him?' asked M. Allou.

'Far less than these ladies, but I did see him two or three times. Besides, their statements don't surprise me. Late yesterday afternoon their cousin was in the vicinity of   Limonest. At least, I thought I recognised him, and I'd be surprised to be wrong.'

The door of the room opened again. M. Allou turned to see the old woman he'd noticed at the rear of the group, and whom he'd forgotten. She approached, and her two canes added a mechanical note to her walk.

'Are you also a relative?' asked the magistrate.

'The aunt,' explained Epicevieille.

When Dorothée reached the corpse she let out a short moan and collapsed. She was caught in time and given a chair.

Hands before her face, she murmured:

'The poor little boy! To end like that! The poor little boy!'

'Do you recognise him?' asked M. Allou.

'Oh, yes!'

29

'Is it your nephew?'

'Yes.'

'Gustave Allevaire?'

'I haven't any others.'

'My aunt!' the Misses Levalois cried out in unison.

And the rebukes started to fly:

'You didn't look properly... It's not Gustave... I can assure you....'

Dorothée uncovered her eyes, stared at the corpse, and covered her face again.

'It's definitely him. There's no possible doubt.'

M. Allou, as can be imagined, was quite embarrassed. He felt that the ex-lawyer offered a better guarantee than the flustered females, so he asked:

'And you, sir, are you confident of your assertion?'

'Well, that's to say... I only saw M. Allevaire two or three times... There was certainly a resemblance... I can't be absolutely sure....'

'But you're certain you saw him yesterday near Limonest?'

'It was quite far away, I might have been wrong.'

'For heaven's sake,' exclaimed M. Allou. 'These contradictions have to be resolved!'

'I can assure you, *monsieur le juge,* that's not Gustave Allevaire,' ventured the inspector from Lyon.

'Why not?'

'He was in Limonest at the time of the crime.' And he proceeded to recount his discoveries of the night before.

'If the anthropometric file is in the hands of the Lyon *Sûreté,* you must have seen his photograph?'

'No, there wasn't time. I was informed by telephone.'

'No matter. They must have it in Marseille. It'll be easy to verify.'

So saying, M. Allou, after bowing to the old women, who had resumed their discussion, left the building accompanied by the deputy public prosecutor.

Shortly thereafter, they arrived at the *Sûreté* and asked to see the Allevaire file.

It didn't require a lengthy examination. Although the victim bore a resemblance to the photograph in front of them, it clearly wasn't the same person.

Furthermore, a comparison of fingerprints confirmed it.

That evening, the Misses Levalois were shown the photograph.

'Ah! This time it's really him,' they exclaimed in perfect unison.

That was also Epicevieille's opinion.

As for the aunt, it proved impossible to get a word out of her.

***

The following day, in his chambers, M. Allou discussed the affair with the deputy public prosecutor.

'At the end of the day,' declared the latter, 'it's pretty simple.'

'Do you really think so?' murmured M. Allou.

'But of course. Someone must have broken into the registry office, removed Allevaire's papers, and was walking around with them. And it just so happened that he was murdered during the same night that the real Allevaire committed the theft. Aren't you convinced, dear colleague?'

M. Allou was shaking his head in doubt.

'Is there something you don't agree with in my explanation?'

'Yes.'

'What?'

'You're talking about chance... and I don't like that.'

'Nevertheless—.'

'It's too simple.'

'Well, do you have a theory of your own?'

'Yes, but it's pure speculation.'

'Can you share it with me?'

'If you wish, my dear fellow. But it's just make-believe. Allevaire, needless to say, never dreamt that he'd left any traces of the theft, let alone irrefutable evidence such as fingerprints. He did think he might be suspected, however, and felt he needed an alibi. Also, with his criminal record, he wanted to live his life under another name. An opportunity arose to satisfy both needs. A murder had been committed, no doubt a settling of accounts by members of the gang to which he belonged. He merely needed to give the victim the identity of Gustave Allevaire. Thus he would officially die and wouldn't be hunted any more, either for the theft in Limonest, or for other crimes he would commit in the future.

'His relatives, he calculated, would be only too eager to identify the body: the aunt out of affection, to shelter him; and his cousins to be rid of him once and for all.

'That's why, on the night of the Limonest theft, someone placed

31

Gustave Allevaire's papers on the body of an unknown person killed in Aubagne. Allevaire himself arranged the hour of the theft to coincide with the execution in Marseille. There wasn't a smidgeon of chance in the whole business.'

'My word,' replied his colleague, 'there's a lot in what you say. I might well accept your hypothesis.'

Just at that moment there was a knock on the door.

'Come in!' said M. Allou. 'Ah, it's you, my dear colleague. What brings you to Marseille?'

The visitor was *Maître* Tissot, a lawyer from Bordeaux, whom M. Allou had met during a criminal matter. Although he had been, as they say in the profession, "on the other side of the barricades," they had established a cordial relationship. *Maître* Tissot, like M. Allou, was a gourmet, as could be seen from his round, ruddy face and jovial demeanour.

'I'm here for a civil case,' he explained, 'and I thought I'd drop by in case you cared for a spot of lunch.'

'Willingly.'

'Are you still very busy?'

'Alas, yes. And this new Allevaire case is likely to deprive me of even more of my leisure time.'

'What about the Allevaire case?' asked *Maître* Tissot. 'You're dreaming, my friend, or else your zeal has carried you away. Why are you involved?'

'Because it happened in my province.'

'Well then, it must extend farther than I thought,' said the lawyer, with a chuckle. 'As far as us, so it seems.'

'What do you mean, as far as you?'

'We're talking about Gustave Allevaire, are we not?'

'Yes, indeed.'

'The same Gustave Allevaire who, in the night of May 9th to 10th....'

'Precisely.'

'... committed, or tried to commit a theft....'

'Yes, a theft.'

'... at one o'clock in the morning....'

'Precisely.'

'... at the residence of M. Clermon, a merchant in Bordeaux?'

32

Chapter V

THE REVELATIONS OF MAÎTRE TISSOT

At the sound of that last word, M. Allou had shaken the table by bringing his fist crashing down on it. The deputy, his eyes popping out of his head, muttered:

'That's the last straw!'

Maître Tissot also expressed surprise—at the impact of his revelation.

'Gentlemen,' he asked, 'how can that minor offence affect you to such a degree?'

M. Allou looked at the stunned faces of the two others, realised that he must have looked just as bemused, and burst out laughing.

'Come now, let's not beat about the bush. My dear *maître*, our surprise is due to an extraordinary stroke of chance. It just so happens that the person you spoke of just now has the same name as another miscreant we're dealing with at the moment.'

'You're sure it's not the same person?'

'Absolutely.'

'Because if you want to be sure, all you have to do is to show me the photograph of your suspect.'

'Do you know this Gustave Allevaire of Bordeaux?'

'Very well. I see him almost every week.'

'My compliments on your relations. You can sniff out potential clients from a long way off, my dear *maître*. Seriously, they can't be the same. Here, take a look at our subject's file, complete with front and side photographs.'

His friend took the box.

'I hate to contradict you,' he said, smilingly, 'but that's him.'

'It's the resemblance that's fooling you.'

'No, he has the same little scar under the eye. I'm as sure of his identity as I am of yours.'

'Listen,' said M. Allou, affecting a serious tone. 'If you're telling me that individual was arrested during that night, either we leave together for the lunatic asylum, or the doctor can choose which one of us he wishes to keep.'

'No,' replied the lawyer, still smiling. 'We won't be reduced to that perilous test, which could cost both of us our liberty. Our Allevaire hasn't been arrested.'

M. Allou breathed a sigh of relief.

'So, my dear *maître*, is it only a suspicion?'

'No, it's a certitude.'

'Why?'

'He was seen inside the house by M. Clermon's secretary.'

'And is that young man prone to visions?'

'I don't think so.'

'Did he look carefully?'

'The man was only a metre away, under the direct light of an electric torch. And he met him practically on a daily basis.'

'Listen, *Maître* Tissot, there's something incomprehensible about this whole business. Do you know the exact depositions of the Bordeaux witnesses?'

'Good Lord! Yes, the whole town is talking about it and confirming what I'd read in the newspaper.'

'Well then, if you have the time, would you be good enough to take me through everything, without omitting any detail?'

'Right at this moment, it's difficult. I have to go back into court. But at lunch, if you like?'

'Agreed.'

***

Impatient though M. Allou was, he didn't neglect to consult the wine list with his customary thoroughness. Once he'd made his choice, he looked at his friend and said:

'I'm listening. Who is this M. Clermon?'

'A successful wine merchant in his thirties. A very energetic individual, intelligent, and with a shrewd business sense. He started from nothing and is now one of the biggest merchants in town. As you know, that kind of business requires a lot of capital, which he accumulated from his own savings: at his age it's a remarkable accomplishment.'

'Remarkable,' agreed M. Allou. 'Is he honest?'

'Scrupulously. There's no better reputation than his.'

'Perfect. Continue. Where does he live?'

34

'He has a townhouse in R... Street. Aside from his domestic staff, his sister and his secretary live there as well.'

'Tell me about them.'

'There's nothing much to say. Marthe Clermon is a pretty enough young woman, well brought up, very serious and, naturally enough, highly sought after. The secretary, Serge Madras, is twenty-five years old: they say he's intelligent and hard-working. That's all I know.'

'And is there anything going on between the two young people?'

'You're asking too much of me. I'm not at that point in Clermon's confidences. In any case that has nothing to do with the story.'

'You can never know in advance, my dear *maître*, what will be of interest and what will not. Anyway, continue. How is Gustave Allevaire involved?'

'Well, *monsieur le juge* ....'

'Please don't address me so formally as I'm about to savour a *dorade grille,* even though I am involved in a criminal case. It ruins the taste. What were you saying?'

'That Gustave Allevaire... that file you showed me this morning doesn't match my recollection of him. I'd been about to tell you that, up until now, he'd been an impeccably honourable man.'

'That must be somewhat of an exaggeration, even for a Bordeaux man talking to a Marseille man.'

'I realise that. But what I can tell you is that, since coming to live in our city a year ago, Allevaire has acquired an excellent reputation.'

'What does he do for a living?'

'Nothing. He was said to be a person of independent means, and he seemed rich enough. I met him often in my circle of friends, and I can assure you I never envisaged him as a client of the magistrate's court. And, furthermore, he was received in the best families. Obviously his wealth counted for a lot: many of the mothers saw him as a future son-in-law. And his appearance certainly inspired confidence.'

'That's a pre-requisite for a top-flight swindler,' observed M. Allou drily.

'True enough. But I've never seen a more sincere face in my life. Even in his anthropometric file, where everyone else looks like a brigand, and you or I would look like candidates for the scaffold, he manages to look like a saint.'

'Quite true.'

'And if you'd seen his smile and the ingenuous look in his blue

35

eyes… Anyway, he was received everywhere, and notably *chez* Clermon. He dined there several nights a week; everything was going swimmingly when, last night—no, excuse me, I slept in the train, which has left me a little disoriented. I meant the night before, the night of May 9th to 10th….'

'Are you quite sure?'

'As sure as I am of your presence here. They talked about nothing else yesterday in Bordeaux. So, as I was saying, at around one o'clock in the morning, the secretary Serge Madras was at work in his office on the first floor.'

'The young man is indeed hard-working.'

'It happens often, it seems. His employer works late and often gives him fresh orders during the evening. He was writing letters, I assume, when, in a nearby room—M. Clermon's office, in fact—he heard a noise. He happened to have a question he wanted to ask of his employer, and so, assuming that the latter hadn't gone to bed, he went in to talk to him.

'Imagine his surprise when he saw that the chandelier wasn't lit and the man standing there was using an electric torch! It was extinguished immediately, but not before Serge Madras had bounded across the room, snatched it from the stranger's hand and shone it in his face. That's when he recognised Gustave Allevaire.

'The other, without putting up a fight, rushed out into the corridor, and the secretary pursued him, starting a hue and cry.

'Marthe Clermon was standing at the door of her room   just as our man ran by.'

'Was the corridor illuminated?' asked M. Allou.

'Yes. The lights are only turned off when the secretary goes to bed.'

'So the young woman had no difficulty in identifying the intruder?'

'That's what one would have assumed, but she claimed he'd gone by too fast, and she was too startled to be sure she recognised him.'

'What did she say, exactly?'

'That it might well have been Gustave Allevaire, and she was almost certain it was—she hadn't seen anything to cause her to doubt it—but, nevertheless, she wasn't prepared to swear to it.'

'Fine. And what about Clermon himself?'

'He only arrived after the intruder had left, and didn't see anything. He was asleep at the time of the theft.'

'Theft? What was stolen?'

'Nothing at all.'

'So the offence doesn't seem very serious,' observed M. Allou with a wry smile.

'Not at all, it's a blatant offence. Two of the desk drawers were forced open. If the fellow didn't take anything, it's only because he didn't find anything of interest. He didn't get the chance, anyway: there were tens of thousands of francs in the third drawer, but he ran out of time.'

'How did he get into the building?'

'Oh, he had ample time during the past year to make a copy of the key, unless he picked the lock.'

'So there was no inside bolt?'

'Yes, but they neglected to use it.'

'Another detail, if you please. Because Allevaire was invited so often, surely he must have known the secretary's habits?'

'Meaning?'

'Meaning his habit of working very late. Why was he reckless enough to attempt his burglary before everyone was asleep? And in the room next to the secretary's office?'

'It wasn't exactly a habit,' clarified *Maître* Tissot. 'I merely said it happened quite often. The other might not have known it: he left around eleven o'clock when he dined there and probably didn't know what happened elsewhere in the house.'

'It's possible. Unlikely, but possible.'

'So what do you make of all that, dear colleague?'

'Well, nothing for now! I'm digesting both your eloquence and this fine cuisine, don't ask me to think as well.'

'So, still just as mysterious.'

'But I can assure you.... Besides, it's all very confusing at the moment. Can't you give me any more details about Serge Madras, the secretary? Where did he come from?'

'He's from a good Bordeaux family, but he's an orphan, the sole remaining member. He must have inherited quite a fortune.'

'So why does he do such menial work?'

'Because he's very young, twenty-five years old at the most, and he's hoping to become M. Clermon's partner, and maybe his brother-in-law as well. You know, a fortune one hasn't worked for is not highly regarded these days.'

'Quite. Well, *maître*, it only remains for me to thank you for your kindness. You've been as clear and precise as you are in court.'

'I'd like to hear the opinion of the tribunal?'

'They're deliberating, my friend, they're deliberating. The wheels of justice grind slowly, as I'm sure you've come to realise.'

'I've never said it of you!' exclaimed *Maître* Tissot.

'Well, you've been wrong, as you can see. *Au revoir*, my dear colleague. I must return to my chambers, where other matters far more banal await me. Thank you for your visit.'

'And thank you for your invitation. I hope to return the favour when next you come to Bordeaux.'

'And who knows?' said M. Allou dreamily. 'That's not entirely out of the question.'

Chapter VI

M. ALLOU'S TEMPTATION

M. Allou had only been back in his chambers for a quarter of an hour when he received a visit from the deputy.

'So, my dear colleague, what did you learn in the course of your lunch?'

'Some curious things.'

And he proceeded to give a detailed account of what he'd been told.

'But that's fantastic!' exclaimed the deputy. 'The man couldn't have been in Bordeaux and Lyon at the same time!'

'I see there's no fooling you.'

'So, how do you explain it? There are more than five hundred kilometres between the two cities!'

'Very simply: because he was in Lyon, he wasn't in Bordeaux.'

'Nevertheless, he was recognised.'

'Yes, someone claimed to have recognised him....'

'Do you think Serge Madras lied?'

'I'm practically sure of it.'

'But why? What was his intention? What was his motive?'

The deputy, when a question troubled him, was in the habit of repeating it in many forms.

'Why?' said M. Allou slowly. 'That is the question.'

'And you haven't found the answer?'

'If it were only that! The problem is I've found two.'

'What are they?'

'Here's the first. Serge Madras wants to hurt Allevaire, for a motive yet to be determined. Perhaps he just senses a dangerous rival.'

'Because of the young woman?'

'Precisely. And, at the same time, because of the partnership he's hoping for with Clermon.'

'So he makes a slanderous accusation against him. Or, rather, he takes advantage of a burglary to denounce his rival? Yes, that must be it, without a doubt.'

M. Allou lit his pipe slowly, and then announced, in a calm voice:

39

'Unfortunately for him, he runs out of luck. Madras makes his accusation on the same night that Gustave Allaire commits a theft—a real one—five hundred kilometres away.'

'Why do you say that in such a sceptical tone?'

'Because, my dear deputy, my statement contained a word I don't like: luck.'

'Ah! That again.'

'Yes, it's my pet subject, I admit. What's more, the theory of the slanderous accusation, which I dutifully presented to you, may very well contain contradictions.'

'Explain yourself.'

'My dear deputy, if Madras was trying to get rid of Allevaire, he must have considered him to be a rival, for whom Marthe had testified evasively. But, if she did in fact have a soft spot for the miscreant, why not simply denounce the lie? After all, the intruder had passed very close to her. If she hadn't recognised him, all she had to do was to say so. But, by her equivocation, she appears not to want to contradict the secretary.'

'Maybe, in her emotional state, she really hadn't seen the man clearly?'

'Perhaps. All I was trying to do was show you the contradictions that arise when you bring luck into the picture. Which leads me to reject—no, let me rephrase that—not to accept automatically my first hypothesis: that of the secretary's hostility towards Allevaire.'

'So you have a second one,' said the deputy. 'Let's hear it.'

'It's the exact opposite, in fact: complicity between the two men.'

'Now you've lost me completely.'

'Allevaire was planning to rob his cousins in Limonest. It seemed like an easy operation. He was very familiar with the premises and knew that he had nothing to fear from the three old women, who wouldn't leave their rooms out of fear. He suspected there might be quite a lot of money in the desk, because he'd seen them occasionally open one of the drawers to pay a supplier. There was also the silver. He'd had plenty of time during his visits to copy the key and to observe that—e ach counting on the other—the two sisters frequently neglected to bolt the door.

'The theft might not be all that fruitful, but there was very little risk. That was vital to Allevaire, with his criminal record. In any case, he needed the money to sustain his lifestyle in Bordeaux, where he probably hadn't had enough opportunities for theft. His pockets were empty and he was counting on his cousins to refill them. Hence the burglary.

'But he might be a suspect, despite everything, and would need to be able to produce an alibi for the night of the theft. He thought of two, but seems to have had difficulty choosing between them.

'The first, and most radical, was his own murder that same night. Once his family recognised the body—and I explained to you this morning why he had every reason to expect they would—nobody would be looking for any other proof, and from then on Allevaire would be presumed dead.

'But, for that to happen, someone would have to be killed. No doubt he knew that, amongst the gang he frequented, one of the members had been singled out to die, and he could take advantage of that murder... but only if the execution took place on the same night. Maybe, at the last minute, he'd had reason to doubt it, and so conceived another alibi.

'It was Serge Madras who would have to provide it. He would let an accomplice into the Clermon townhouse and pretend to discover him and identify him....'

'But that would be like going from Scylla to Charybdis!' exclaimed the deputy. 'In order to avoid being suspected of the burglary of his cousins, he planned to get arrested for burglary of the Clermons!'

'Not at all, my dear colleague. You're forgetting that nothing was stolen from the Clermons.'

'But the mere attempt is equally bad in the eyes of the law.'

'Yes, and enough to keep the police occupied for a while and deflect suspicion from the Limonest theft. When interest in that has died down, Serge Madras will, little by little, change his attitude: either he'll start to have doubts about his accusation and say he's no longer sure to have recognised the culprit: or trivialise the theft, saying it was only a portrait of the young woman that was stolen.'

'But, speaking of the young woman, your previous objection is still valid. Why didn't she denounce the lie if she hadn't, in fact, recognised Allevaire? Unless you suspect her to be part of the gang as well?'

'I don't think so, or she would have been less hesitant in her accusation. No: quite simply she didn't want to contradict the secretary, because she's in love with him. So she stuck to her evasive

41

deposition.'

'Even supposing that to be true, wouldn't it have been simpler for Serge Madras, instead of going through all that taradiddle, to have simply declared he'd run into Allevaire in Bordeaux the night of the Limonest theft?'

'That wouldn't have had the same weight as an accusation. And someone might have suspected a collusion between the two men, and followed that trail. In any case, given that Allevaire, for good reason, hadn't spent the evening with the Clermons, where would the secretary have seen him? He would have had to arrange a late-night sortie, which would have astonished his employer and scandalised the young woman.'

'True enough. So Allevaire had planned two alibis: one in Aubagne and the other in Bordeaux. But it was sheer madness to establish them for the same time! One alibi by itself is precious, but two are fatal!'

'You can be sure,' explained M. Allou, 'that he planned things otherwise. I assume he thought about the Aubagne alibi first. Everything was in place: the man charged with carrying out the murder had the papers ready to place them on the corpse. Then, at the last moment Allevaire learns that, for some reason, the execution has been delayed. That's when he organises the other alibi with Madras.

'But the information was faulty and the murder took place after all. The man responsible, unaware of the precautions Allevaire has taken, carries out his orders to the letter and places the identification papers on the body. And that's how our poor miscreant finds himself with a double alibi for the same night. By sheer bad luck, he gets caught out in Limonest!'

'Well that's certainly a trail worth following,' murmured the deputy.

'Yes, far more than the simple theft of some silverware. There's an entire gang to be discovered—well-organised and with no compunction about dispatching any member they can't trust. What a catch that would be!'

M. Allou's bright, hard eyes gleamed like those of a hunter whose prey was getting near.

'Don't get too excited,' counselled his colleague. 'The entire organisation is in Bordeaux, outside your province, so you won't be the one following the trail. Oh, I know there'll be some ramifications involving Marseille—the "Black House" was obviously a place for rendezvous, maybe even a warehouse for stolen goods—but the central hub of the case is still Bordeaux.'

M. Allou fell silent for a few minutes. Then his eyes started gleaming anew.

'My dear deputy,' he said, 'there may be other possible theories.'

'That's what I was thinking. Maybe—and this is probably your thinking as well—maybe we've been wrong in thinking the Lyon theft was an established fact. Maybe it was an artful piece of stage management.'

M. Allou smiled.

'Explain your thinking. Are you saying that Misses Levalois, or even Aunt Dorothée, knowing that Allevaire's crime was going to be committed here, or that he was going to commit theft in Bordeaux, arranged an alibi in Limonest for him?'

'No!' exclaimed his colleague. 'That would have been stupid. In the first place, they're peaceful people with an excellent reputation, according to the inspector. Allevaire would never have asked them for their help, and they would never have given it. Secondly, Limonest was far more serious than Bordeaux—a theft had actually been committed, so that alibi would have been disastrous for the miscreant.'

'So what do you think happened?' asked M. Allou.

'That maybe the slanderous accusation occurred at Limonest. The two sisters wanted their aunt's inheritance and, to rule her nephew out of the picture, organised the theft of the silverware she loved so much. During a prior visit, they'd kept a spoon which their cousin had touched, and that's how his fingerprints were found on it.'

M. Allou was still smiling.

'So that way we may assume that Allevaire was in Aubagne that night, that it was he who killed the unknown gang member and, to avoid suspicion, placed his own wallet on the victim? Thus gaining the additional advantage of being presumed dead?'

'Yes, but he could equally have committed the theft in Bordeaux.'

'So what you're saying is that either Allevaire arranged an alibi in Aubagne for his theft in Bordeaux or, conversely, an alibi in Bordeaux for the murder in Aubagne? And that, in either case, by an extraordinary coincidence, his cousins fabricated the scene in Limonest?'

'Yes, that's it. Unlike you, I'm not averse to chance.'

43

'I only resign myself to it out of desperation.'

'So you reject my solution?'

'No.'

'Well, that's a change!'

'At least, not officially. On the contrary, I'll happily accept it and charge Allevaire with murder. Do you see any consequences?'

'Quite a few,' replied the other.

'There's one that interests me more than any other. Legally, I'll have seized on the most serious crime to charge him with: the thefts in Bordeaux and Lyon pale in comparison. And, since the crimes are connected, I can ask the public prosecutors in both places to cede authority in my favour. That way, I'd be in charge of everything.'

'Obviously,' murmured the deputy, 'I can but admire your zeal. But, however clairvoyant you may be—and I yield to no one in my admiration of your powers—do you really believe justice is best served that way? As you yourself have said, the central nub of the affair is Bordeaux, and your colleague on the spot there seems better placed than you to discover the truth.'

'Maybe you're right. I'll have to think about it. Good day to you.'

***

But M. Allou didn't reflect on the matter for long.

Slowly his eye wandered along the dusty shelves which decorated the walls and lingered on the boring files lying in disorder on the table.

'All this paperwork,' he murmured. 'What am I doing here stuck with this mess?'

He'd chosen his profession in the hope of satisfying his two great passions: logic and adventure. He hadn't been too disappointed about the first, having solved numerous interesting problems which rose above the daily grind. As for the second, it had been a disaster: more and more he felt his title of civil servant weighing on him.

Worst of all, he had tasted adventure: he'd allowed himself to be led along in the case of the pearl necklace, then those affairs in Eguille and Meillerie. At present, his resistance to temptation was weak.

'Action,' he said to himself. 'Direct action, without paperwork.'

For a few seconds he stared at the telephone, then picked it up. The switchboard operator came on the line. The die had been cast.

'Get me the public prosecutors of Bordeaux and Lyon urgently,' he ordered, 'and then the *Sûreté* in Paris.'

A few minutes later, the first communication was established.

He had no difficultly persuading his colleagues to defer to him on both cases.

To the *Sûreté* he explained that, because the cases involved small towns remotely situated, he needed assistance from Paris and specifically requested Superintendent Sallent.

The two had worked together on the case of the magic necklace and Sallent always obeyed him blindly, whatever he decided.

'Send him to Bordeaux,' he said. 'There's an inspector from Marseille there who can bring him up to speed... Yes, tomorrow morning at eight o'clock, in the Café Centrale... agreed, then.'

He hung up just as the deputy entered.

'Have you come to a decision?' asked the other.

'Yes. Two, even.'

'What are they?'

'The first is to take control. My colleagues have agreed.'

'Well, you certainly don't shirk responsibility! What's the other one?'

'To take two weeks' vacation.'

The deputy stood there for several seconds with his mouth open, then departed, telling anyone who would listen that his poor colleague did in fact need rest, and not just for two weeks. For a few months, more likely, or even years, alas!

46

Chapter VII

IN BORDEAUX

In Bordeaux, Superintendent Sallent was waiting on the terrace of the Café Centrale.

He was a beanpole, as tall and thin as Epicevieille, but much younger. He had the same bony face but not the same expression: it reflected energy, not compunction.

The superintendent was a good policeman, methodical, thoughtful, very thorough in his searches, and possessed of a magnificent courage. As for his intelligence, it was barely above average, and the more gifted of his colleagues joked about it amongst themselves.

A silent type, Sallent never sought the limelight, with the result that many underestimated him. But M. Allou understood him and appreciated his solid qualities. It was to Sallent's skill, precision and *sang-froid* that the magistrate owed his life during the affair of the necklace, and he never forgot it.

As for the superintendent, his admiration for M. Allou knew no bounds.

Nonetheless, as he sipped his beer that morning, he did allow himself a slight criticism.

"Highly intelligent people are often forgetful," he told himself. "M. Allou asked me to meet an inspector I've never seen… Couldn't he at least have given me a description? There's a customer over there who looks as though he might be waiting for someone as well."

But suddenly he saw someone standing in front of him, smiling.

'You, *monsieur le juge!*'

'Sh! Here I'm not a magistrate, my dear Sallent. You can call me Dupont.'

'Very well,' said Sallent, without further discussion. 'But I can't see the inspector from Marseille whom I'm supposed to meet.'

'Yes you can. He's right in front of you. His name's Dupont.'

'But it's you, *mon*—.'

'Sh! Yes, it is. More precisely, I'm one of your collaborators from Paris: Inspector Dupont.'

'But it's—.'

'A seizure of power? I know, and I don't want to impose such a complication on you. If you have the slightest misgiving about it, I'll take the next train back to Marseille.'

'Oh, *monsieur le* ... M. Dupont, you can order me to do anything.'

'I'm not ordering you.'

'You're asking me. For me, it's the same thing.'

'Thank you, Sallent, that's very kind of you.'

'Not at all. I would never miss the opportunity to work with you.'

'I think it could be interesting. We're dealing with people who are well organised and ruthless with regard to anyone with a loose tongue.'

'Thank you for having chosen me!' exclaimed Sallent enthusiastically.

'There's not a minute to lose. We need to get in touch with the Bordeaux police. But please don't call me "*M. le juge*," or even "M. Dupont," but simply "Dupont."'

'I'll try, but it won't be easy.'

'Try.'

'Yes.'

'Say: "Yes, Dupont."'

'Yes, Du... Dupont,' stammered the superintendent.

'It doesn't trip easily off the tongue, but that will come. Phone the local *Sûreté* and tell them you've made contact.'

***

After that, M. Allou brought his collaborator up to speed. Sallent listened attentively, nodding his head and forcing himself to say, from time to time:

'Yes, Dupont. I understand, Dupont.'

It was only at the end that he risked a personal observation:

'It's a very strange business. It's lucky you're here... Dupont.'

Shortly thereafter, they arrived at the offices of the local *Sûreté*.

They were made to wait in one of the innumerable rooms, all the size of a prison cell, each furnished with a table and four chairs.

Suddenly the door opened and was completely blocked by a massive square shape. Inspector Protilato's body, hands, face and head were all square.

He introduced himself with a deep chuckle:

'Needless to say, you can call me "Proto," like everyone else. My name's so long that, when someone calls me, they no longer need me by the time they've finished pronouncing it.'

He had a magnificent accent and expansive gestures, which contrasted strongly with the reserve of his visitors. When they only responded with weak smiles, the inspector added:

'I'm not quite sure why you've been sent here.'

Fearing that the man might be offended, M. Allou hastened to explain:

'It's a principle of the Marseille examining magistrate: when a case involves several regions, he enlists the *police mobile*, which speeds up searches considerably. But I don't doubt that in Bordeaux you would have arrived—.'

'Would have arrived?' interrupted Proto. 'I *have* arrived!'

'And what have you concluded?'

'As soon as I heard what had happened elsewhere, it wasn't very difficult to understand. It was a slanderous accusation on the part of Serge Madras, motivated by jealousy.'

'Do you have any information in support of that?'

'No, but all you need to do is think. If Allevaire was in Lyon, he wasn't here.'

'Don't you believe in complicity between the two of them to create an alibi for the culprit?' asked M. Allou.

'You're talking nonsense, my friend. How they do complicate things in Paris! Serge Madras is a bit vindictive, I agree, but apart from that he's perfectly honest. He doesn't belong to any gangs.'

'Didn't everyone believe the same of Allevaire before this business happened?'

'Yes, but Madras is from around here.'

'Yes, of course, that's a guarantee.'

Proto turned to Sallent:

'Believe me, superintendent, sir, there's nothing to be found in this town. It's a very banal affair. Take a few days off and relax. A short break will do you a world of good, especially beside the sea, at this time of year. Visit the coast, there are some delightful spots. And if I can be of help in any way, just let me know. I know all the cheap restaurants.'

Sallent gave an indistinct grunt. M. Allou replied on his behalf:

'It's an excellent idea. Nonetheless, to justify our expenses, we'll need to go through a few formalities: a visit to the Clermon townhouse and a conversation with his secretary, that's all.'

'You're right.'

'Just one more question, if I may. It takes at least nine hours by car to reach either Marseille or Lyon. The three offences which have been attributed to Allevaire all took place on the night of the 9th to 10th, at exactly the same hour. So, if by chance he was seen here less than nine hours before the theft Madras accuses him of, then it's the Bordeaux account which will be the true one.'

'Nobody saw him here,' declared Proto.

'Are you sure? Did you conduct a thorough investigation?'

'Very thorough, as always.'

'What did they say in Clermon's house?'

'Nothing, there was no one there.'

'A man in his situation without domestic staff?'

'Your question surprises me,' replied Proto. 'You're aware that his situation was a façade, I assume? He spent as little as possible on his residence, and his apartment, even though it was in a top location, was only looked after by one cleaning woman. She saw him at nine o'clock in the morning, fifteen hours before the events. He would have had all the time in the world to take a train.'

'Quite so. Anything interesting in the house?'

'Nothing at all."

'Thank you, my friend.'

Proto left, shaking their hands as he departed, and giving them three restaurant addresses.

'I've prepared a rogatory letter requesting judicial assistance,' M. Allou told his partner. 'Hurry up and get it subdelegated by an examining magistrate and we'll breathe in the air of the Clermon residence.'

'Mustn't count too much on Proto,' growled the superintendent.

'Quite. But we can't afford to vex him, he could be useful.'

'Don't you believe in a slanderous accusation, Dupont?'

'I don't know. Everything's possible. I hate to admit there are such things as coincidences, but they do occur sometimes.'

'If I understand correctly,' said Sallent, 'that's why you questioned Proto. You asked him whether the theft here wasn't the real one, and the one in Limonest, coincidentally, had been stage managed?'

'Exactly. Even though I hate to admit there's such a thing as chance, I would have been prepared to accept it if Allevaire had been seen in Bordeaux shortly before the fateful night. But it didn't happen, so I come back to the only theory which rules out coincidence: the miscreant manufactured two successive alibis to cover the theft at Limonest which, by clumsiness or excessive haste, ended up covering the same exact time.'

'That certainly seems to be the most likely,' said Sallent.

'All the same,' continued M. Allou, 'we can't afford to stick to one single point of view. The situation in Bordeaux could just be a slanderous accusation and not collusion. The first thing we have to establish is this: is Madras Allevaire's enemy or his friend? In fact, stubborn though Proto is, he could be helpful. I'll put him in charge of keeping an eye on Madras. Obviously, he'll become suspicious if he is indeed an accomplice. But who knows? He thinks he's not a suspect, so he might get careless.'

They sought out the inspector and Sallent conveyed M. Allou's request, adding:

'Pointless, obviously... Well aware... Necessary for report... Understand?... Paperwork.'

Proto shrugged his shoulders in resignation.

'You can count on me,' he said. 'Might as well do that as anything else. But you'll have to explain it to my boss. He'll accuse me of wasting my time.'

Chapter VIII

A PECULIAR FIANCÉE

By eleven o'clock, M. Allou and Sallent were in Clermon's office.

He was a young man with alert eyes in a thin face. He received the visitors cordially, without exuberance or reserve.

'Gentlemen,' he said, 'I'll obviously help you as much as I can, but I'm afraid I won't be of much help. I didn't see anything and don't know anything more than you do.'

'You can at least provide some basic facts,' replied M. Allou. 'First of all, are you absolutely sure nothing was stolen?'

'Absolutely. As you would expect, I checked everything with great care. Besides, the two drawers that were damaged contained only business papers, of no interest to anyone but myself.'

'But in the third, or so I've been told, the intruder could have found money?'

'Yes, ten thousand francs, money I leave there permanently, in order to pay small bills without opening the safe or writing a check.'

'Is your secretary aware of that?'

'Certainly.'

'Very well. So we can eliminate one hypothesis.'

'Which one?'

'That he helped himself by means of an accomplice, in order to pull the wool over our eyes.'

'Are you suggesting he was looking to rob me of ten thousand francs?'

'I was, but I recognise that it doesn't hold water. He would have broken into the third drawer, because he knew it was there.'

M. Allou had only raised the possibility in order to get the merchant to speak spontaneously about his secretary, and the tactic had worked perfectly.

'No, gentlemen, that accusation must be refuted, not just for the reason you cited, but because of Serge Madras's character. First of all, I consider him to be perfectly honest. And secondly, with his fortune, he wouldn't be interested in such a small sum.'

'You never know. A gambling debt... an expensive mistress....'

'He leads an exemplary life and thinks only of his job.'

'Still, you don't follow him around.'

'He hardly ever leaves here, and never at night. His work takes up all his time, so he never gets to go outside.'

M. Allou smiled.

'I admire him for consecrating all his waking hours to you. Is it entirely because of your conversation?'

It was Clermon's turn to smile.

'I understand what you're suggesting. But don't you think your question is indiscreet?'

'I've often been accused of that during my career.'

'Well,' continued Clermon, laughing out loud. 'I can't hide it from you, I've already said too much. You're right, if Serge never leaves here, it's not just because of me. I gather you're aware I have a young sister.'

'And why would you conceal your secretary's feelings?' responded M. Allou indulgently. 'From what you say, you couldn't wish for a better marriage for Miss Clermon?'

'There's no doubt about it.'

'Then forgive me for having for one moment suspected your future brother-in-law of theft...'

M. Allou waited impatiently for the response to his obvious insinuation. He'd just learnt that Madras loved the young woman, which corroborated the hypothesis of the slanderous accusation. But that would have been pointless if Marthe Clermon loved Serge in return, which would mean Allevaire wasn't a dangerous rival after all.

Concealing his avid interest, M. Allou put on his most innocent expression and left the question hanging in the air.

'I don't see why I shouldn't reveal the project,' replied the merchant. 'It's not yet official, and I wouldn't want you to announce it before I've had the chance to tell my friends. That said....'

'The proposal has been made and accepted,' concluded M. Allou.

'Yes, and the ring will be placed on her finger in a few days.'

'I'm overjoyed for the future bride.'

'You're too kind.'

'A reciprocal feeling is so important,' M. Allou continued persistently, looking for a more precise confirmation. 'It's so sad when a young woman is resigned to a marriage.'

'Happily, that's not the case. My sister is as eager as her fiancé.'

Clermon replied amiably enough, but was perplexed by such sentimental considerations coming from a police inspector. He told himself ironically that it took all sorts to make a world.

'Yes,' continued M. Allou, 'I'm so glad that the circumstances didn't spoil the young woman's dream.'

'The circumstances?'

'Surely you know about the accusation made about her fiancé? A slanderous accusation is something quite serious.'

'But I don't believe a word of it!' exclaimed the merchant.

'So, do you think he really recognised Allevaire?'

'No, obviously not, but he thought, in good faith, that he did.'

'The error seems difficult to believe. He saw the man close up and in the beam of an electric torch.'

Clermon smiled indulgently.

'At least, that's what he says.'

'Don't you believe him?'

'Frankly, no. I get the impression that he embellished his role in order to impress his fiancée. As soon as he set foot in my office, the burglar ran off, and he ran after him. He didn't walk up to him, as he claims.'

'Is this a supposition on your part, or did he confide in you?'

'Oh, it's pure supposition. He would never confess to his boast, even if he were about to be hanged. So, having only seen the man from behind, he could have been mistaken. And, because he didn't like Allevaire much, his suspicions—.'

'He didn't like him very much?' asked M. Allou casually.

'No. People in love are so sensitive. He accused Allevaire of wooing my sister and he was jealous.'

'Nevertheless, if Miss Clermon's sentiments....'

'One doesn't reason in these matters. He didn't like him, and that's that. Maybe he was more sensitive than I was and guessed the true nature of that odious individual.'

'You have full confidence in him?'

'Oh, absolutely! When you arrest Allevaire and look at his face, you'll be hard pressed to believe he's a confidence trickster.'

'Thank you for the information. Might I speak to Miss Clermon now?'

'Is that really necessary? She's been quite shaken by the events, and

55

she's already been questioned by the examining magistrate. I'd prefer her to be left alone.'

'I understand your concern,' continued M. Allou, with a gentle stubbornness. 'But we're obliged to do so for our report... Rest assured, we'll be as brief as possible. And, to intimidate her less, I'll do it myself, one on one. My colleague will not be present.'

Sallent, who hadn't said a word so far, got up.

'I'll meet you in the restaurant,' M. Allou told him. 'Wait for me.'

After the superintendent had left, he continued:

'Where can I meet your sister?'

'Here. I'll call her in.'

'No, the rules say that witnesses must be questioned separately. In the present case that's pointless, I agree. But rules are rules, it's not up to us.'

Clermon had pressed a button and a servant entered.

'Show the inspector to the salon and ask my sister to join him.'

***

Whilst contemplating the Louis XVI furniture, which included some spectacular pieces, M. Allou was thinking hard.

If the feelings of the two young people were indeed reciprocal, the theory of the slanderous accusation would have to be abandoned. It was far too serious a charge to have been levelled as the result of a bad mood.

That would leave the theory of complicity, or mere boastfulness, as Clermon had suggested.

There was no time to ponder the matter further, because the door was opening.

Marthe Clermon was indeed pretty, as *Maître* Tissot had told him. Not exactly beautiful, for her features were not regular enough, but nice to look at, with her big blue eyes, turned up nose, and slender but curvaceous figure. She looked sixteen, even though she was much older.

But it wasn't just her pleasing appearance which caused M. Allou to stare at her. He was observing something else. The smile on her lips was tense and there was no corresponding light in her eyes. Her eyelids were reddened.

Embarrassed by the examination—M. Allou's stare was always hard and disquieting—Marthe Clermon fiddled with a ribbon of her blouse and attempted to accentuate her smile.

'Why are you smiling?' demanded M. Allou brutally.

'B-because....'

Her entire face tensed and all traces of forced joy vanished.

'Because you want to appear happy? My dear child, at my age one is not fooled so easily.'

Now he was speaking in a gentle voice.

'You're not very good at pretence, miss, and I congratulate you for that. Please sit down. You've been crying, haven't you? Don't try to deny it, I can see it quite clearly. You've been crying and you're going to cry a lot more....'

Marthe couldn't restrain herself; two tears ran down her cheeks and she started to sob. M. Allou clutched the arm of his chair, which was a sign of intense emotion on his part.

"I'm a brute," he said to himself. "I'm about to exploit her grief... it's odious of me."

He was on the point of standing up and calling off the questioning, when he controlled himself.

"No," he said to himself, "I'm as implacable as a surgeon. The very fact that this child is unhappy means that I can't abandon her."

He continued in a loud voice:

'I was expecting more joy from a fiancée.'

She didn't reply, but the tears started to flow more quickly.

'You are engaged, aren't you?'

She shook her head gently.

'I was led to believe so by your brother. He wants it very much, it seems.'

She nodded her head.

'And what about you?'

This time she burst into tears, with her head in her hands.

'Listen to me, child, I'm old enough to be your father. You mustn't, under any circumstances, allow yourself to be pushed into marriage. Don't be afraid of me, I'll defend you. If you need my help, don't hesitate to ask.'

Sobbing convulsively, she didn't reply.

M. Allou left the room quietly.

***

Out in the street, he walked slowly.

It was obvious to him that Serge Madras was a despicable individual. Doubtless his money was necessary to the success of Clermon's business. According to *Maître* Tissot, he'd started out with minimal capital and must have found himself in trouble at a time when credit was limited.

Madras hadn't hesitated to take advantage of the situation and made his financial help contingent upon marriage to a young woman who didn't love him, but was willing to sacrifice herself to help her brother. It was the most ignoble of bargains and had to be stopped at all costs.

But what was the best way to reach Madras?

Was he Allevaire's enemy or his friend?

Once in the restaurant, he explained his thoughts to the ever-placid Sallent. He knew he could count on the other's frankness. But Sallent listened to him in silence, raising no objection and not favouring one hypothesis over the other.

'What I need to do now,' concluded M. Allou, 'is to meet Serge Madras. I'll try not to show my hand, so as not to put him on guard. I'll see him after lunch. This time you'll come with me, for it would be good to for you to make his acquaintance.'

Chapter IX

SERGE MADRAS

At around half past two they once again rang the door bell of the Clermon townhouse and asked to see Serge Madras. They were led directly to his office.

M. Allou entered first and stood still for a moment, such was his surprise. Even though experience teaches magistrates not to trust first impressions—the most ignoble scoundrels can have deceptive appearances—and despite the current example of Allevaire, M. Allou, like everyone else, believed in his subconscious that character was reflected in the face.

And he'd never seen a face more frank and open than that of Serge Madras. The blue eyes that looked straight at him, candidly and even naïvely; the fine features, rounded but energetic; the well-modulated voice; all corresponded so little to what M. Allou subconsciously expected that he stood still momentarily.

He recovered quickly, cursing himself for being influenced by an impression. He introduced himself with the cordiality he'd already decided to show, but which was now incontestably less painful than he'd feared.

'I'm happy to make your acquaintance. M. Clermon has spoken about you in the most flattering terms.'

'He's too kind, don't believe the half of it. But please be seated, gentlemen. I fear your visit will be a disappointment, for I've racked my brain in vain but can't find anything to add to my original deposition.'

He expressed himself so frankly, and with so much ease, that it was becoming difficult to ask him questions. M. Allou adopted his most paternal attitude, and began:

'How—.'

The young man interrupted him.

'How did the events transpire? It's very simple. It was one o'clock in the morning and I was working here, at this table, when I heard a noise in the next room, which is my employer's office. I thought he must not have gone to bed, so, because I needed some information, I went in. There was a man in there rifling the drawers, with a small torch in his hand which he extinguished immediately. I grabbed it from him and shone it in his face long enough to take a good look. I tried to detain him, but I had only one hand because the other was holding the lamp. He ran off and I pursued him in vain.'

M. Allou finally managed to get a word in.

'That wasn't my question. I was about to ask how you explained a man being in Bordeaux and Lyon at the same time.'

'There's no doubt, gentlemen, that I was mistaken. It must have been just an extraordinary resemblance.'

'I find that hard to accept. One can be mistaken about someone one hardly knows, or only glimpses. But you've just confirmed that wasn't the case. You said you got a long look at him: several seconds.'

'Excuse me,' interjected Sallent. 'I read your deposition this morning, when I visited the examining magistrate, the one you made just a few hours after the incident. Those were your exact words.'

'Then I misspoke. Several seconds seems highly improbable: the man wouldn't have stayed still for that long. I wanted to say I got a good look at him and my words were imprecise.'

The retraction rekindled M. Allou's suspicions.

'Even if it's only for a moment, one can recognise someone,' he replied.

'Maybe the man was made up to look like Allevaire?'

'No, that won't wash. Maybe a professional actor could imitate a silhouette by the clothes, the hair and the posture. But Allevaire had only added a small blond moustache, so his face would not have deceived someone so close to him.'

'You do agree that I was mistaken, however,' retorted Madras rather curtly.

'I find that surprising.'

'Are you thinking, by chance, that he wasn't in Lyon that night, but here?'

'No, that's not what I'm thinking.'

'What, then?'

M. Allou remembered just in time that he'd resolved not to give the young man cause for concern. He adopted an anxious tone in his response:

'I'm beginning to wonder whether it wasn't a double, which would complicate matters enormously.'

His tone had been so natural that Sallent looked at him in surprise. The superintendent knew that, even though a resemblance could fool someone who scarcely knew a person, it could not fool someone who saw them every day.

'I can well believe it,' declared Madras, nevertheless.

'And perhaps,' continued M. Allou, 'you didn't look at him quite as attentively as you claimed.'

'What do you mean?'

'Listen, I promise not to repeat anything. Your account suggests considerable courage on your part. Maybe, in reality, it was somewhat less, and you only got a look at him from behind.'

'I won't allow anyone to doubt my word on that point!' exclaimed Madras brusquely, getting to his feet.

'Very well, I won't press the matter. One last piece of information: with whom did Allevaire associate?'

'In our circle he saw a lot of people.'

And he rattled off a list of fifteen or so names.

'And outside your circle?'

'Outside? I don't know. I only saw him here.'

'You didn't like him, then?'

'No,' replied Madras tersely.

'The impressions aren't justified.'

'Come now... a little jealousy perhaps?'

'No, that would have been stupid.'

'Are you sure of his sister's feelings towards you?'

'Sir, do not abuse your authority by insulting me. If I hadn't been sure, would have I asked for her hand in marriage and would she have accepted?'

His indignation appeared extraordinarily natural, which was exactly what M. Allou wanted by way of reassurance. He himself had questioned the young woman, which served as the touchstone with which to measure Madras's capacity for lying.

Which appeared to be formidable.

'We've finished,' announced the magistrate. 'Would you be good enough to tell M. Clermon we'd like to see him again?'

Without a word the young man got up and went into the adjacent room.

'About the double—,' began Sallent rapidly.

'I know,' said M. Allou, cutting him off.

'Think he didn't see the man's face but will never admit it.'

'He seems courageous, my dear superintendent.'

'Can't trust appearances,' growled Sallent.

Madras came back into the room.

'You can go in, gentlemen,' he said curtly.

And, without another word, he sat down.

***

M. Allou put on his most benign face.

'Excuse me for troubling you again, M. Clermon,' he said. 'I forgot to ask you for a piece of information this morning. With whom did Allevaire associate?'

'Oh, he inspired confidence in everyone in our circle.'

'I know. And outside?'

'Outside? I don't quite see....'

'Who was his closest friend?'

'I was, undoubtedly.'

'You've never seen him with anyone suspicious?'

'Well, maybe, but suspicious is too strong a word.'

'Please explain.'

'I've seen him a couple of times with Le Borgne.' (1)

'Le Borgne?'

'It's a nickname. His real name is... wait a minute... Etrillat, I think. But nobody ever calls him anything else, because he does only have one eye, as the result of an accident.'

'Who is he?'

'A wine broker.'

'And what is he accused of?'

'Nothing. Only laziness. He works irregularly and people think he's not serious. I suggested to Allevaire, by the way—being a stranger to the town, he couldn't have known—that he would be lowering himself if he continued. I was naïve: now it seems it was the contrary.'

'Thank you.'

(1) le borgne = the one-eyed man

M. Allou stood up. He looked Clermon straight in the eye and, maintaining his most naïve tone, said:

'By the way, I spoke to your sister. Her happiness is a joy to behold....'

'Isn't it?' replied the other, with a beatific smile.

For once in his life, M. Allou was disconcerted by the cynicism of someone. He found himself lost for words and left.

***

Once in the street, his anger exploded.

'No one has ever mocked me so brazenly!' he exclaimed. 'Did you hear that "Isn't it?" said with a straight face, Sallent? If you'd seen that poor girl this morning....'

'Should probably excuse him,' said the superintendent.

'Excuse who?'

'Clermon. And also Serge Madras.'

'I don't understand.'

'If the girl's in love with Allevaire, they're doing everything they can to hide it. Afraid of scandal. Prefer to make believe engaged to secretary.'

'Your sentences aren't very long,' said M. Allou, 'but they're full of good sense. Hell's Bells! What you say is very plausible... In which case, Madras wouldn't be the cynical liar I took him for.'

'Mustn't judge appearances,' growled Sallent.

'Meaning what? Come, my dear superintendent, what are your impressions?'

'Never impressions on a case.'

'Decidedly, Sallent, you've a hundred times more common sense than I do.'

'Means nothing without intelligence.'

'Come, come!'

'Know myself well. Next to you, imbecile. Find many things. Don't know what to do about them.'

'You're being too modest, Sallent. In any case, your observations are better than mine.'

'Possible. You're often distracted. Notice anything now?'

'No.'

'Café terrace, over there.'

There were thirty or so customers seated at tables and M. Allou scanned them all. It took him more than a minute to recognise the massively square inspector Proto.

'What! He's there doing nothing, when we were counting on him to watch Madras. I'll tell him a thing or two!'

M. Allou started towards the terrace. Sallent restrained him by the arm.

'Mustn't talk to him here.'

'Why not?'

'See who's sitting nearby?'

M. Allou looked at the tables again and saw nothing out of the ordinary.

'Behind him,' explained Sallent. 'Thin young man with long face?'

'I don't recognise him.'

'His eyes?'

'Sallent, you're speaking in riddles.'

'One of them's not moving. Only one eye.'

'You're incredible. Nothing escapes you. Now, there's no proof that he's that friend of Allevaire... whatsisname....'

'Etrillat,' said the superintendent.

'Yes, Etrillat.'

'When in doubt, be careful. Better for him not to see us. *Zut*, too late, Proto has seen us.'

The inspector had, in fact, stood up and was waving his arms in a manner which they couldn't pretend not to see.

'Too bad,' said M. Allou. 'Let's go over there, but not to sit down.'

They walked towards the café.

'So,' shouted Proto when they were fifteen metres away, 'we ignore our friends now?'

'I wasn't sure it was you,' replied M. Allou when he reached the table. 'I thought you'd be elsewhere.'

'If there are any observations to be made, it's for the superintendent to say, not you. You may be a Parisian, but you're only an inspector like me, with all due respect. Now we've settled accounts, what'll it be? You do have a minute, don't you, superintendent, sir?'

'No,' replied Sallent. 'After lunch I always go for a walk.'

'In this heat? Well then, I'll come with you.'

He paid for his drinks and followed them.

'I thought,' said Sallent, when they were out of earshot, 'that you were supposed to be watching Madras?'

'But I can't spend the whole day in front of the house.'

'Obviously. But I thought you'd be replaced by a colleague if you took a break.'

'I thought about it. But, to be frank about it, superintendent, sir, it all seems such a waste of time.'

'Not for you to judge,' cut in Sallent. 'Can have your chief order you to do it, if necessary.'

'All right, all right. But here in Bordeaux we don't like make-work. *Au revoir.*'

'Wait. Who was sitting behind you on the terrace?'

'Behind me?'

'Try to think. Young man with glass eye.'

'Oh, him. A wine broker, Etrillat.'

'Anything to tell about him?'

'Nothing, superintendent, sir. You seem to suspect everybody.'

'That's my business. Does he work?'

'Not much, I believe. But I don't know much about him.'

'Then find out. And discreetly.'

'You can count on me.'

'As far as discretion goes, that remains to be seen. Start by not shouting our names and titles on café terraces.'

'I didn't shout.'

'Right. That's your natural voice. And the accent.'

'So I don't have a Paris accent like you. You do what you can.'

'Don't get upset. And keep a sharp eye out. *Au revoir.*'

'*Au revoir.*'

'What an imbecile they've stuck us with,' continued Sallent, after the inspector had left.

'If he could at least agree to work,' said M. Allou, smiling. 'Until he's given us his report, we're at a loose end. I can't see anything to do this afternoon but take a walk. Fortunately, there's a lot to see in this town.'

And they set out for the Saint-André cathedral.

Chapter X

A STRANGE DISCOVERY

That evening, after dinner in the hotel dining room, M. Allou and Sallent sat down to read. At eleven o'clock, Sallent stood up and folded the newspaper he'd been reading.

'I'm going to bed,' he announced. 'All that walking has tired me out.'

'Me too. At least we got to see some beautiful monuments.'

'Better that than nothing,' growled Sallent unenthusiastically.

'Console yourself. Proto is sure to tell us something tomorrow.'

'Do you think so?'

'One must always go to bed in a state of optimism. Let's try to persuade ourselves that, this very night, he'll find something.'

'Tonight? He'll be sleeping,' retorted the superintendent.

'Do you really think so?'

'If we want to find something out about Madras, we'll have to do it ourselves.'

'But where would we find cover?'

'Didn't you notice that small square with thick bushes thirty metres from Clermon's townhouse?'

'I'd forgotten.'

'Dupont, as you insist on calling yourself, you'd be useless as an inspector. Let's go!'

***

Shortly thereafter, they arrived at the square. It was immediately obvious that all the streets were deserted and that Proto was nowhere to be seen.

'That useless pig!' exclaimed Sallent.

'Maybe he's following Madras somewhere in town?'

'Don't you believe it. He's asleep somewhere. Let's hide.'

They climbed over the gate of the small garden and found a dark corner, from which they could see the entire length of R … street where Clermon's townhouse was situated. The night was overcast but quite warm.

'Not very well lit, this area,' observed Sallent.

They waited. M. Allou dared not smoke and suffered in silence. A nearby clock chimed midnight, then one o'clock, then two o'clock.

'We're being totally ridiculous,' announced M. Allou suddenly. 'Nothing's going to happen. We're better off in bed. I'm going to light my pipe, for a start.'

'Don't do things by halves,' retorted Sallent. 'Surveillance started must be finished. Don't move. Put away your matches. The job's the job.'

Ten minutes later, they saw a figure in the distance, walking towards them.

'Is that Madras?' asked M. Allou.

'I've no idea. I've never seen him in the street. I wouldn't recognise his walk. These wretched gas lamps don't provide any light.'

There was nothing unusual about the man's walk. It wasn't the moment for them to show themselves. If he had something to hide, he would run away if he saw two silhouettes suddenly emerge from the garden. They had to wait for him to get closer.

Now he was fifty metres away... then forty. They could make out a hat rammed down over his eyes, casting a dim shadow over his face.

Thirty metres at most... He was drawing level with the Clermon townhouse... He looked around, stopped dead and knocked three times on the door so lightly that M. Allou couldn't hear. The door opened immediately and the man went inside.

'Damn!' said Sallent. 'That was quick.'

'Did you recognise him?'

'No. It could have been Madras or anyone else.'

'We'll know soon enough. If no one comes out again, it was him. But I'd be surprised.'

'Why?'

'He must have a key. He doesn't need anyone else to open the door for him.'

'Good point. Let's wait. It's a quarter past two... We need to be ready to pounce when he comes out again. But we mustn't leave the garden: he could see us and become suspicious.'

The wait only lasted five minutes and ended more eventfully than the two watchers had expected.

The door opened so abruptly that M. Allou and Sallent, sensing something abnormal and throwing all caution to the winds, had jumped over the garden gate and were running towards the house.

The unknown man came out at the same time. He appeared to be trying to escape, but in the direction from which the detectives were coming. In his panic, he only spotted them when they were ten metres away, when he made an abrupt turn and sped off in the other direction.

But, because he was no longer wearing his hat and had turned right below a gas lamp, his face had been perfectly visible.

'Allevaire!' shouted Sallent.

He only knew him from the photographs in his file, which M. Allou had sent him. But that was all he needed to be sure he was right.

Needless to say, they ran after the fugitive. As they reached the townhouse, they saw someone in the doorway: it was Clermon. But they didn't stop and continued in hot pursuit.

Allevaire appeared athletic and not about to let himself be captured.

'Stop or I'll fire!' shouted Sallent.

But the threat was in vain. The man had arrived at a narrow cross street. They could only watch him turn and disappear out of sight. Pursuit being futile, they stopped, out of breath.

'He came back. Of all the nerve!' exclaimed M. Allou.

'That's because we assumed he was on the run: there's no town where they're less likely to be looking for him than here.'

'True enough. What the devil was he doing *chez* Clermon?'

'Well soon find out,' said Sallent. 'In any case, if he was indeed welcomed here, it didn't last very long. Did you see his face?'

'Yes, he seemed to be bleeding.'

'I'll say. From the lip and the nose. He must have been thumped pretty hard!'

'Let's hurry,' said M. Allou. 'The first thing is to alert the *Sûreté*.'

***

They found Clermon in front of the door, waiting for them in his dressing-gown.

'Telephone?' asked M. Allou.

'Here.'

The magistrate rapidly notified the *Sûreté* of the criminal's presence in the town, in order for the stations, the roads and the port to be watched.

That precaution taken, he returned to the vestibule where he noticed the bruises on the man's face.

'What happened?' he asked.

'That villain got in again!' exclaimed Clermon. 'Did he escape?'

'Yes. How did you discover his presence?'

'I heard a noise in my office. I was asleep, but it woke me up immediately. Did you know my bedroom was next door?'

'No, I didn't.'

'Yes, on the side opposite my secretary's office. Mine is right in the middle of the house. I suddenly remembered I'd left my safe open; it doesn't happen very often, because I keep bonds there and sometimes large sums of money. As I went in, I could see the man methodically searching my desk. Luckily it has several drawers. Doubtless the cash interested Allevaire more than the bonds—difficult to get rid of—which is why his search was taking so long.'

'Well, you've certainly explained that very well,' muttered M. Allou. 'Now can I see the safe?'

'We need to go upstairs. Follow me.'

M. Allou and Sallent followed him into the office.

The safe was indeed open. M. Allou noted that the drawers were all shut and opened one or two of them.

'Your thief is a very careful man,' he observed. 'There's no disorder. All the stacks are intact. And, most curious of all, he didn't bother to take the money immediately to hand, on the shelf. It seems to be quite a large amount, which ought to have satisfied him. What do you think?' he added sharply, turning suddenly to face Clermon.

'Me? Nothing at all. It's not for me to judge his methods.'

There was a certain curtness in his tone, all the more surprising because of his normal affability.

'Let's go over your account again. So you heard a noise?'

'I only took the time to put on a dressing-gown.'

'You weren't armed?'

'I don't possess a revolver. I went into the office and saw a man with an electric torch going through the contents of the safe. I went for him and punched him right in the face. But he's well-built and didn't fall down. He retaliated and hit me in the eye, as you can see. Then I hit him again. The fight didn't last long, and he fled.

'I tried to go after him, but in vain. That's all I can tell you, gentlemen.'

'What temerity!' murmured M. Allou, in a strange tone of voice. 'Two theft attempts so close together. This villain is truly dangerous... nothing stops him.'

Clermon didn't reply.

Sallent had been listening attentively, his eyes glued to the floor. Slowly, he made his way to the corridor and beckoned to M. Allou to join him.

'The traces of blood don't begin until the staircase,' he said quietly. 'And not a single piece of furniture was disturbed in the office.'

'I noticed that,' replied M. Allou, 'and the same is true for the safe. One part of the story is true, but the fight didn't take place where he said it did.'

He went back into the office.

'Sit down, please,' he said. 'The facts may be more serious than you think. Do you know how Allevaire got into the building?'

'The same way as before, I assume: with a false key.'

'No, someone opened the door for him.'

The blood drained from Clermon's face and he turned as white as a sheet.

'Are you sure?' he asked in a hoarse voice.

He got up slowly.

'Absolutely sure. I saw it with my own eyes.'

The other hesitated for a second, then murmured:

'Who was it?'

'I couldn't see. Could it have been one of the servants?'

'I don't believe so. They're old and were thirty years with their previous employer. Do you want to talk to them?'

'There's no point. I wouldn't learn anything from their denials. Besides, *everyone will deny it*, so it's useless for me to talk to any of them.'

'You're right.'

'... But I'll make an exception for your sister, who may have heard something.'

'No, I beg of you, it's quite useless. If she'd heard even the slightest noise she would have called out or rung the bell. It's better that she doesn't know... at her age and in her emotional state... particularly at night... I assure you it's not a good idea.'

Clermon, normally so sure of himself, was babbling. M. Allou had the distinct impression that an energetic interrogation of Marthe

71

would lead to a confession.

Nevertheless, he dared not do it. Such brutality towards a young woman revolted him in advance.

Slowly, he walked to the door.

'You have to question her,' murmured Sallent.

M. Allou shook his head.

He thought for a moment, then turned to Clermon:

'After all, this is your business. Nothing was stolen. If you don't file a complaint....'

'Why would I? I settled his account myself. Let's not talk about it. We don't need another scandal.'

'Agreed. The file is closed. *Au revoir.*'

***

As soon as they were in the street, Sallent started to grumble.

'Why didn't you question the girl?'

'I don't know.'

'She's the one who opened the door and she would have admitted it.'

'You seem so sure, Sallent. But don't jump to conclusions. Madras bothers me much more than she does.'

'I don't believe a word of it. If you really thought so, you'd have questioned the girl.'

'I'm not saying it wasn't her, just that I'm not certain. In any case, I didn't want to risk extracting that confession in front of her brother.'

'You mustn't be so pure. The job's the job, for heaven's sake!'

'Forgive me for coming along, Sallent. I've hindered you more than I've helped.'

'Don't worry about that. I know that, in the end, you're the one I can count on. Proto's the one who's going to get it in the neck. That animal! We were counting on him....'

Chapter XI

THE SHOT

The following morning, at eight o'clock, Sallent was already on the telephone. His impatience had awakened him, despite the late hour he'd gone to bed.

'Hello? Is that the *Sûreté* ? Is Inspecteur Proto there? Do you think so? Well send him over to my hotel. Yes, urgently.'

And the superintendent paced up and down the lobby whilst waiting for him.

A quarter of an hour later, the inspector was there. Sallent looked around to make sure the room was empty, then planted himself in front of Proto. The contrast was almost comical: the tall, thin superintendent and the short, wide inspector with the bulging eyes.

'Ah, there you are, M. Proto.'

'What's happening?'

'Nothing. I'm eager to hear the results of your investigations last night. You were on duty?'

'Yes, superintendent, sir. I watched the Clermon residence, where Madras was staying, the whole night.'

'The whole night! That's very good. You don't seem at all tired.'

'I'm used to it.'

'Doubtless. And what did you observe?'

'Absolutely nothing. As I predicted, Madras never went out and there wasn't the slightest incident.'

'Really? Not the slightest? It's disappointing when zeal like yours goes unrewarded. But, no matter, the effort is what counts. You can be sure I'll speak to your superiors about you....'

Had Proto begun to detect the irony? He seemed to become more anxious, and asked:

'And you, superintendent, sir, did you find anything out? I'm told at the *Sûreté* that you spotted Allevaire, and I know there's an order out to watch the roads and the station. You're quite sure it was him?'

'Yes, my lad. But with a detective like yourself, he'll be caught quickly. Do you have any information about Etrillat, otherwise

73

known as Le Borgne?'

'I devoted my afternoon to watching him while you went for a walk.'

'You're tireless. And what did you find?'

'Not much....'

'You astonish me.'

'Because there wasn't much to find! He doesn't work much, makes a little bit on the cards, and travels occasionally for his work. Nothing unfavourable.'

'That's all? Really, it's a pleasure working with you. Now get some sleep, you must need it. *Au revoir*. And don't be overzealous.'

Sallent turned his back on the inspector without shaking his hand. He growled between clenched teeth:

'If only M. Allou hadn't pledged his silence to Clermon, this idiot would have got a real telling-off. The best place for a nitwit like this is the Monaco Museum.'

'Have you eaten?'

It was the voice of M. Allou, who was coming down the stairs.

'No, I'm not hungry.'

'You seem in a bad mood?'

'Not surprising! Not only do you stop me interrogating, but also from dressing someone down when it's needed. If it weren't you giving the orders....'

***

The dreary weather didn't do anything to help the superintendent's mood. He wandered off on his own to take a walk, in the vague and admittedly stupid hope of running into Allevaire. Needless to say, it didn't happen.

That evening, at around seven o'clock, he found M. Allou in the restaurant, and sat down opposite him without saying a word.

'Still upset, Sallent?'

'Yes... should have questioned the girl.'

'You really won't let it go?'

'The job's the job.'

'Even in front of her brother?'

'I didn't ask that.'

'Well, listen, I'll call now. If she's alone, we'll go over there.'

'Better late than never.'

M. Allou swallowed his food hastily and went to the telephone.

He came back to tell Sallent that Clermon would be out until eight o'clock and the girl would be available before then.

Sallent had already put his hat on.

'Would have been better last night.'

'Stop grumbling. I'm trying to make you happy.'

A quarter of an hour later they arrived in the vicinity of the Clermon residence. In the middle of the dark street, a massive silhouette stood out, not moving.

'That imbecile!' shouted Sallent. 'Standing in the middle of the road like a street lamp.'

The superintendent did not have a gift for imagery.

Sallent advanced towards the inspector, who, staring up at the façade, didn't see him coming.

'Oh, excuse me, my boy. You were so well hidden I couldn't see you.'

'For goodness sake, superintendent, sir, after your remarks this morning, I wanted to make sure you could see me working.'

'Congratulations! Is Madras in the house?'

'No, superintendent, sir.'

'No? Then what the hell are you doing here?'

'I started to follow him this afternoon. I lost him around four o'clock.'

'Now why doesn't that surprise me? Do you think he did it on purpose?'

'I don't know. He got into a taxi and there weren't any others around. That's not really my fault. I couldn't run after him. My legs aren't as long as yours. So, I thought the best thing to do was to come back here. But he hasn't been back for dinner.'

'All right, but let's get back onto the pavement, or we're going to get run over.'

A taxi had, in fact, come into the street. They approached the townhouse and, to their surprise, the taxi drew up next to them.

Serge Madras got out.

'Ah, there you are! I've just come from your hotel and I also phoned the *Sûreté*. I couldn't even find Inspector Proto.'

'That's the last straw,' growled Sallent. 'He has to follow his own inspector!'

'So, what's happening?' asked M. Allou.

'I'll tell you in a moment.'

Madras paid the driver and turned to the three men:

'I think I've found Allevaire's hideout.'

'Are you sure?' asked M. Allou.

'Pretty well.'

'But how...?'

'I'll explain. I was sitting in the taxi just after four o'clock when I noticed Le Borgne on the pavement in front of me. M. Clermon has mentioned him, I believe?'

'That's right.'

'Allevaire was an acquaintance of his. But I noticed something strange: as my taxi drew level, he turned his head away, as if he didn't want to be recognised. I was sure he'd seen me, and he knows me well enough; I've done business with him. His attitude seemed strange, so I told the taxi to stop and got out. I managed to follow him without being seen.'

'You must have been very careful,' observed Sallent. 'Shadowing someone who's suspicious isn't easy.'

'Anyway, I managed to stay on his tail until we reached the outskirts. He turned into a narrow street, so I stopped at the corner, naturally. I'd done it a few times already and then had had to run to catch up. I watched him walk casually along the street. Then I saw him stop suddenly in front of one of the houses, thrust a piece of paper into the letter box, and proceed as if nothing had happened. That's when I left and came to find you.'

'Interesting,' said M. Allou. 'It might not be Allevaire, but we have to check. What kind of building is it?'

'Small, two storeys. It's in a working-class neighbourhood. The back of the house must overlook waste land.'

At that moment, a luxury two-seater drew up.

'Well, well! I've arrived in the middle of a council of war.'

The speaker was Clermon.

'What's happening, gentlemen?' he added, getting out of the car.

They quickly brought him up to speed.

'I'm only sorry I can't drive you there,' he said. 'This car is too small and the other one has a flat tyre....'

'We'll take a taxi.'

'At this time of night, there are very few passing by. It's best to call for one; there's a telephone in the vestibule.'

'I'll take care of it,' said Proto.

He went inside and emerged a few minutes later to announce there was one on the way.

'I'll come with you,' declared Madras. 'I can point the house out to you. At night the numbers are almost impossible to read.'

'All right.'

M. Allou took a few steps to one side, and the superintendent joined him.

'This will be a waste of our time,' whispered M. Allou.

'Do you think so?'

'That's my guess. Madras is trying to allay our suspicions by offering to help. How he must be mocking us at this moment. I'm almost tempted not to go.'

'We have to, all the same,' replied the superintendent. 'We can't afford to miss an opportunity.' Then he added, inevitably, his favourite slogan:

'The job's the job.'

'You're right. Let's go.'

The taxi arrived and they set off.

***

The streets were empty at that time of night and they made good progress. After a few minutes, Madras announced:

'We're almost there. Perhaps it would be better to get out here.'

They paid the driver and proceeded on foot. Soon they arrived at a squalid side street.

'Here we are,' said Madras, pointing. 'The house is fifty metres down the street from the corner.'

'Very well,' said M. Allou. 'Let's take a look.'

They avoided getting too close to the other houses on that side of the street, so as not to be seen from the windows.

They reached the door without incident. A small copper bell hung above it; beneath it was a piece of cardboard attached with drawing-pins. Getting closer, M. Allou was able to read what was written on it, despite the darkness:

"Mrs.Tapire. Ring once."

Presumably the ground floor tenant. They could see there was a light on.

To get into the building, it was obviously preferable to count on her, rather than Allevaire, who presumably lived on the first floor.

M. Allou pressed the bell once and it rang feebly. He stood waiting for a woman to open the door and was taken off guard by what happened next.

The door was flung open suddenly, just as the bell started to ring. And, before anyone could distinguish anything in the dark corridor, a man rushed past M. Allou and Sallent, who were closest to the doorway. He turned to his right; Madras, who was to his left, was unable to stop him. Proto, on the other side, could have stopped the fugitive, but was so surprised that all he could do was gesticulate feebly.

The man already had a lead of ten metres. Despite his speed, Sallent had recognised him: it was indeed Allevaire. They all threw themselves into the pursuit.

There was no point in ordering him to stop or they would shoot. They'd said that the night before, and he'd taken no notice.

M. Allou noted, once again, that the villain had a remarkable turn of speed. Even Sallent, despite his long legs, lost ground. In the group, only Madras was able to keep up. Soon, he was forty metres in front of the others—which wasn't a surprise; the young man was well built and obviously did a lot of sport.

At first, Madras wasn't able to narrow the gap. But gradually, due to his age advantage and greater stamina than the older man, he managed to lay a hand on the other's shoulder. He was, by then, sixty metres ahead of the group.

Suddenly the fugitive stopped dead, turned, and dealt Madras a tremendous blow to the temple. M. Allou had the time to see that the man's hand was not bare, but was fitted with a brass knuckle-duster.

Madras crashed to the ground.

Without hesitation, Sallent drew his revolver. He was about to fire at the man's legs and would certainly not have missed—for he was an excellent shot—but Allevaire, at that very instant, reached another corner and ducked out of sight.

When the pursuers eventually reached the corner, there was no one in sight, and they abandoned their pursuit.

Sallent took out his frustration on Proto.

'You should have stopped him when he ran straight by you.'

'You too, superintendent, sir.'

'No,' retorted the other, 'Dupont and I were too close to the door and couldn't help but be surprised. You, on the other hand, were two metres away and had time to react. You were scared, weren't you?'

'Never! I've never been afraid. Just didn't keep a clear head, just like you.'

'Let's take care of the wounded first,' chided M. Allou.

Madras lay on the ground, his face covered with blood.

Sallent leant over the body to examine the wound. He had acquired quite bit of medical knowledge over the years.

'There's no skull fracture,' he announced, 'but it was a close thing. The skin's been broken and there's lots of blood, but he'll recover quickly.'

'Since the wound isn't serious,' said M. Allou, 'we can leave him with Proto. As soon as he recovers consciousness, take him to the nearest police station by taxi,' he ordered the inspector. 'We have work to do; I want to take a look at his lodgings.'

'Won't you be needing me anymore?' asked the inspector.

'No. Really,' growled Sallent.

He left with M. Allou.

'That wasn't a fake blow,' declared the other.

'Definitely not.'

'Since the two men don't appear to be colluding, we'll have to drop that theory. If Madras accused him of theft, it wasn't to give himself an alibi, but to get rid of a dangerous rival. Allevaire has just taken his revenge.'

'That's what I think, too,' replied Sallent.

'And, if Madras tried to get him arrested that night, it was less to help us than to get rid of a menace who worried him. If he could get Allevaire sent to Guyane, the young man needn't fear his vengeance.'

They had arrived at the door of the house. It was still open, but now it was illuminated and they could see an old woman.

'Mrs. Tapire, no doubt?' asked M. Allou.

'Yes, sir, was it you who rang?'

'Yes, indeed.'

'When I opened the door, I didn't see anyone there. I looked in the street, and I saw a bunch of people pursuing another one. So I went back into the corridor.'

'Do you know who the fugitive was?'

'My word, sir, since I found the door open, I thought it might be the upstairs lodger.'

'Do you know him?'

79

'Barely. I do housecleaning all day long, and I've only seen him three times.'

'Has he been living here a long time?'

'About six months. That's when they installed the telephone.'

'Oh, he has a telephone?'

'Yes, gentlemen.'

'And can you hear it ring?'

'Yes, when I'm in the house.'

'Obviously,' groaned the superintendent.

'Tonight, did you hear the phone ring?' continued M. Allou.

'Yes, gentlemen, five minutes before you got here.'

M. Allou took Sallent to one side.

'Just checking if I remember correctly. The taxi took about four minutes go get here from R…street?'

'Correct.'

'Tell me, my good woman, do you mean five minutes exactly? Did you look at the clock?'

'Oh, no, sir, I said "five minutes" in a manner of speaking.'

'So it could have been three?'

'Or seven or eight. Roughly five.'

'Good. One last question: what's the name of the owner of the building?'

'M. Allevaire.'

'What did you say?'

'I said: M. Allevaire: A, double L—.'

'Yes, yes. What's the lodger's name?'

'Gustave, simply. I've seen letters in that name in the box.'

'And to whom do you pay your rent?'

'To a bank collector, who comes with a bill.'

'And how did you find your lodgings?'

'Through an agency.'

'Whose owner you've never seen, I suppose?'

'Never.'

'At least, as far as you know….'

'I swear to it!'

'You must never swear to anything. *Au revoir*, my good lady.'

Leaving her speechless with his parting words, they began to climb the stairs.

'Someone alerted him,' growled Sallent.

'There's no doubt. And just before our arrival. Thirty seconds later and we'd have got him.'

They stopped on the landing.

'I think we blundered,' said the superintendent.

'How?'

'We listened to Madras's account beneath the windows of the Clermon house. That was idiotic.'

'I agree,' admitted M. Allou. 'But we couldn't have known what that young man was about to tell us.'

'Nevertheless, you should never talk about anything when you could be overheard. It was even more careless when we knew who would be in the house, because you'd just made an appointment.'

'You're thinking of Miss Clermon.'

'Of course. I can't think of anyone else. Can you?'

'I agree,' murmured M. Allou.

'You're still indulgent.'

'What can I say? She acted out of love.'

'That's not a reason,' growled Sallent. 'Anyway, there's no doubt where the call came from.'

'Let's go,' said M. Allou, putting an end to the discussion. 'Let's see what we find in his room. Not much, I'll bet.'

'And furthermore, the door isn't even locked. Let's go in anyway, if only out of curiosity.'

They entered a small vestibule of no more than three metres square, from which opened two other rooms.

The first, which overlooked the street, was a kitchen. They could see that it was frequently used, but there was almost no furniture. There was nothing to see there.

They went into the second room, which overlooked the waste land behind the house. It also had been lived in. There were a few pieces of furniture: a bed, a table, a bowl, a wardrobe, and a few chairs. The only luxury—or was it a precaution?—was a pair of tulle curtains, thick enough to hide the lodger during the daytime. A pair of interior shutters, currently open, performed the same function at night.

The two men had made all those observations from the doorway, by means of the single light in the vestibule, without switching on the bedroom light.

The superintendent pressed the switch and went into the bedroom.

He had only taken five paces when the glass of one of the windows

81

exploded, and the sound of a bullet whistled in his ear. Out of instinct, he ducked.

Someone had fired on him from outside, from the waste land.

Chapter XII

THE UNEXPECTED VISITOR

Sallent's reflexes were those of boldness, not caution. Without thinking, he bounded to the window, opened it, and looked out. It was stupid: he could see nothing in the night and was offering himself as a target.

Luckily, M. Allou, particularly when it came to others, acted more sagely in times of danger. At the very moment the superintendent was showing himself at the window, his companion switched the light off, plunging the room into darkness once again.

Sallent, abandoning the idea of seeing anything outside, returned to the back of the room.

'You probably saved my life,' he said.

'Yes, and I was probably wrong. There are already too many idiots like you.'

'Oh, *monsieur le juge,* in the case of the necklace, you did much worse.'

And they chuckled together at the memory.

'So, we're equal,' said M. Allou. 'But our man's becoming dangerous, by heaven! According to the police reports, he limits himself to thefts and is as meek as a lamb. But last night he attacked Clermon. And tonight he knocked Madras out and fired on us... By the way, has poor Madras regained consciousness?'

'I can assure you, it wasn't serious.'

'I was just checking. You know, you can see the whole street from the kitchen, if you lean out of the window. I'm going to take a look.'

'Stick your head out so he can get a clear shot,' mocked Sallent. 'Here, let me do it.'

'Excuse me, it was my idea.'

And M. Allou leant out as he'd said he would. The street was absolutely deserted. The wounded man must have regained consciousness.

'Perfect,' he declared. 'You see, no one fired on me. Besides, it would have been much more risky from the street.'

'What the devil has he got against us?' asked Sallent, after a few seconds. 'Is he afraid of our perspicacity? That would be flattering, but the results we've obtained so far don't justify it. Could it be, *monsieur le juge,* that he's guessed who you really are?'

The superintendent was being serious. M. Allou looked at him and smiled.

'I'm rather inclined to think that he forgot some compromising article as he was fleeing, and is afraid we'll find it. So therefore we must look for it. But, before we do so, there's a precaution we have to take.'

'What might that be?'

'You'll see.'

M. Allou went into the bedroom, shut the window, and closed the shutters.

'There,' he said, 'that's better.'

'Decidedly,' growled Sallent, 'you must think I'm useless.'

'We're dividing the work: you opened them, I shut them. But I was smart enough to do it with the lights out.'

'Your presence can be detected anyway, from the movement of the windows.'

'It had to be done. I was beginning to get nervous. Now we can switch on the lights.'

Once again the room was illuminated.

'We'll examine everything,' continued M. Allou. 'I'll take the wardrobe. Meanwhile, you slit open the mattress and the pillow. After that, we'll dismantle the furniture.'

They had been working for less than five minutes when Sallent suddenly stopped, making a sign to M. Allou not to move. He listened attentively, then murmured under his breath:

'Someone just came into the building.'

'Yes, I heard them. They're coming upstairs.'

'What a nerve! Well, if he wants to meet me, I'll be happy to oblige.'

And Sallent, after turning off the light, drew his revolver.

'I left mine at the hotel,' whispered M. Allou.

'Naturally, you never do anything otherwise. Luckily, mine will be enough. Take my electric torch. Shush!'

There was absolute silence except for the sound of the doorknob of the entrance door turning cautiously. A moment later, someone entered the vestibule.

Sallent couldn't contain himself. He should have waited until the intruder reached the bedroom, which would have been less dangerous. But he flung open the door whilst M. Allou, at the same time, switched on the torch.

There was no need for the superintendent to fire. The man had immediately raised his arms. At the same time, they recognised the long face: it was Etrillat, nicknamed Le Borgne.

'What are you doing here?' asked M. Allou.

'I must have mistaken the house,' replied the other.

'That's odd. Your key seems to fit the door downstairs.'

'That's how I made the mistake.'

'Enough of the nonsense,' growled Sallent. 'You're in deep trouble, my lad. Let's look in your pockets.'

He searched carefully, but could find no weapon or anything else of interest.

'Did you come in alone?' he asked next. 'Be careful how you reply. If I find an accomplice on the stairs, you might well take a stray bullet.'

'I'm alone.'

'I'll double check,' said M. Allou. 'Yes, it's my job because I'm holding the lamp.'

He shone it on the stairs and the vestibule below. There was no one hiding there.

He came back in, turned on the lights and announced, while filling his pipe:

'We're going to have a little chat, M. Etrillat, because you've been kind enough to pay us a visit.'

'I'm not much one for talking, I prefer to play cards.'

'Alas! There aren't any cards in the house. Admittedly I haven't searched everywhere. But we can discover other interesting things instead. Would you like to help us with our enquiries, M. Etrillat?'

'No, I'm tired,'

'It's not nice to leave us to do all the work. For I assume that you, too, are looking for something?'

'Thank you, I don't need anything.'

'You didn't drop by just out of curiosity? Tell me what you're looking for and I'd be delighted to help you find it.'

'A bottle of cognac.'

85

'You're too modest. I'm going to search this place, and I'm sure I'm going to find something more interesting than that. All I ask is that you keep your hands behind your back. And, to assist you in that, the superintendent will tie them together with that rope over there in the corner.'

Sallent promptly executed the order.

'Now,' continued M. Allou, 'make yourself comfortable on that chair in the middle of the room. And please be patient, we'll do our best to be quick.'

They resumed their search. Whilst Sallent was checking the mattress, M. Allou, who had already unfolded all the linen on the shelves, now took them down.

Next, they stripped the straw seating from the chairs, and the superintendent examined the tiles on the walls, one by one.

Etrillat watched the two men impassively, but there was a mocking gleam in his good eye. Occasionally he smiled.

'Take your jackets off,' he said after a while, 'or you'll catch cold when you leave.'

The superintendent frowned. He felt ridiculous. All their efforts appeared to be in vain: they'd found nothing.

'But, instead of knocking ourselves out,' exclaimed Sallent suddenly, 'we should look at the last piece of furniture.'

'There's another one?' asked M. Allou in astonishment.

'Not here. In the vestibule. You didn't notice?'

'No'

'Naturally! The large coat hanger?'

'Of course! Look behind it. It won't take long, anyway.'

Sallent went into the vestibule and moved the coat hanger away from the wall. His face lit up in a broad smile:

'Here we are!' he exclaimed, bending down.

An object which had previously been jammed between the hanger and the wall had just fallen to the floor. It was a wallet.

The superintendent picked it up and turned to Etrillat. The latter's expression had changed and it appeared that any inclination to joke had disappeared.

'What's this?' asked Sallent.

'I've no idea. Why don't you take a look?' replied the other, his tone now bitter.

The superintendent inspected his discovery and seemed

86

disappointed. All it contained was a few papers and a driving licence, all in the name of Pierre Fumage. The name meant nothing to the policeman.

'Fake papers, no doubt,' he observed.

M. Allou had moved closer to take a look. Suddenly he seized the driving licence and stared at it.

'I've seen that face before,' he said, after a while.

'Where?' asked Sallent.

'I can't remember. I'm certain I've seen it... but the name doesn't ring a bell... Wait! I've got it!'

'Who is it?'

'That fellow who was murdered in Aubagne! Who was carrying Allevaire's papers!'

'Hell's bells!' gasped Sallent. 'What a discovery!'

M. Allou turned to Le Borgne.

'What were you going to do with this?'

'I don't know what you're talking about. Someone was killed in Aubagne?'

'Stop wasting our time. You came here to find the wallet.'

'And what exactly would I have done with it?'

'I don't know. Taken it so we couldn't find it, maybe.'

'I didn't even know about it until now.'

'What did you come here for? No more joking, please. I don't have the time.'

'Ah, well, I might as well tell you the truth because it's all going wrong. Allevaire owed me five thousand francs and I wanted to demand them.'

'It's ten o'clock at night, not a good time to come.'

'He wouldn't let me come earlier for fear of being seen.'

'How did you get hold of the downstairs key?'

'He gave it to me, so I could get in without waking the old witch on the ground floor.'

'So you've come here often?'

'Often enough, I admit. Allevaire was a good friend. It wasn't up to me to tell you where he lived.'

'He's been here a long time?'

'About six months. His official address was in town, but he used to come here every night to pick up the important stuff.'

'If he didn't sleep here, how did you manage to meet him at such a

87

late hour?'

'I would drop a note in the box before seven o'clock. He'd find it and then come back later. That's what I did today, although in the circumstances I assume he's not coming. I wanted to be sure to meet him because of the five thousand francs, which I needed.'

'Why didn't you admit all that at the beginning?'

'I had no reason to tell you anything about him. It was the discovery of the wallet which changed my mind. I sensed that everything was going wrong.'

'That much is true,' growled Sallent.

He didn't believe a word of the story, which he judged to have been invented on the spot. What troubled him was that M. Allou seemed to believe it.

During the interrogation, the magistrate's tone had become softer and softer, until now there was no harshness in his voice at all.

Sallent's irritation reached its peak when he heard the witness being asked, gently:

'Have you've told me the truth?'

'Oh, yes, sir.'

'Will you swear to it?'

Frustrated, the superintendent was on the point of intervening, but refrained from doing so out of respect for his colleague.

'I swear!' exclaimed Le Borgne.

'Obviously, we can't reproach you for not betraying a friend. Anyone would have done the same in your position. But you have a poor choice of associates....'

'Whom I remain faithful to in adversity!' exclaimed Etrillat grandiloquently.

Sallent shot M. Allou a reproachful look, but when he saw the audacious and thoughtful gleam in the other's eyes, he bit his tongue.

Without saying a word, he undid the rope.

'*Au revoir*, Etrillat,' said M. Allou in conclusion. 'Forgive us for subjecting you to this treatment, but we didn't know everything at the start.'

This time, it was too much! M. Allou was excusing himself. Sallent, indignant, clenched his fists inside his pockets.

'I don't begrudge you,' replied Le Borgne. 'You behaved quite correctly. Anyone can make a mistake. *Au revoir.*'

And, after bowing slightly, he left. Hardly had the door closed when Sallent, beside himself, made a move to follow him. M. Allou restrained him by the arm.

'But don't you understand?' exclaimed the superintendent. 'He's played us for fools.'

'Do you really think he was the one who fired on us just now?'

'No, of course not. I'm not that stupid. He wouldn't have come into the lion's den afterwards if he had. No, it was Allevaire who fired, to try to stop us finding the wallet. Having failed to kill me, he sent his accomplice over to retrieve it. Le Borgne was hoping that, whilst we were occupied in the bedroom, we wouldn't hear him slip into the vestibule. And if by chance we caught him, he would run less of a risk than Allevaire himself. He could tell whatever story he wanted! It's true—and this is the weak point of my theory—that he couldn't have counted on a credulity like yours. That's very rare.'

The superintendent ran out of breath and stopped. M. Allou, whose hand had been on the telephone, profited from the silence to make a call to the *Sûreté*. He was given the home number of the chief and Sallent, stupefied, didn't say another word.

'The head of the *Sûreté*, please.'

'Speaking.'

'I'm Superintendent Sallent,' said M. Allou. 'Tell me please: don't you have a more capable inspector than Proto?'

'Quite a few, but we put him on that case because it appeared to be straightforward.'

'Very well. Could you supply two men who are adept at trailing suspects?'

'Of course. Who are we talking about?'

'Etrillat, nickname Le Borgne. I've managed to allay his suspicions, but we have to be careful nonetheless. If the operation is well executed, it could lead us to the hiding place of Allevaire.'

'Really? Are you sure?'

'Almost sure. If the surveillance starts immediately. Speaking of which, is it in place for the stations, roads and the port?'

'The stations and the port, yes. The roads are more difficult. There are a lot of them, we don't have enough personnel, and they block the circulation of traffic. If we were talking about a murderer, we could deploy more. But for a mere thief....'

'Yes, quite.'

'Furthermore, Allevaire doesn't own a car.'

'He could easily steal one. The same goes for Le Borgne. Make sure one of your men has a motorbike at the ready.'

'Don't you think he's already left?'

'I don't think so. He's just met up with Allevaire and won't see him again until he has something to tell him or supplies to take him. We mustn't lose time establishing surveillance of his residence.'

'I'll get on it right away. *Au revoir*, superintendent.'

'*Au revoir, chef.*'

M. Allou hung up.

'I'm a prize idiot,' exclaimed Sallent. 'Of course you were right. It would have been pointless to arrest Le Borgne, he would never have talked. Whereas now, he might be useful.'

'Don't get carried away, Sallent, you're not an idiot. Your explication just now seems very likely: Etrillat was trying to retrieve the wallet that Allevaire forgot.'

'It wasn't difficult to work out. What troubles me more is how it got here and why Allevaire had it. I thought he had absolutely nothing to do with that crime,'

'Absolutely is a big word,' replied M. Allou.

'What I meant was he had nothing to do with the actual execution. Naturally, he knew it was going to happen, because he provided the papers that were placed on the victim.'

'And he also asked for the victim's papers in return.'

'Then why didn't he carry them on him?'

'That would have been dangerous until the authorities gave up on identifying the dead man. He was waiting for the case to be closed.'

'Right. Well, at least we now know the victim.'

'Only his name. Otherwise we know very little, apart from the fact that he lived in Grenoble, at the address given on his papers. Tomorrow we'll send them a telegram to learn more.'

'Don't you think, M. Dupont—I have to get used to calling you that—we should have tried to arrest Allevaire last night, by the roadblocks?'

'No, it was too late. A car is easily stolen and surveillance measures take a while to be put into place. Furthermore, he may not have travelled far. Look, as far as tonight is concerned, there's only one thing left to do: go to bed. We need it, after all these watches.'

'Don't you think we should still watch Clermon's townhouse?'

'No. Proto is getting serious. He understands now that laziness has its consequences. He and a colleague are mounting guard. Clumsily, perhaps, but they're there.'

'Maybe we should check on the way back.'

'If you insist.'

They left on foot, and in R...Street they could see a man pacing backwards and forwards on the pavement, whilst keeping a distance from Clermon's townhouse.

'You see?' said M. Allou, smiling, 'he's making progress. Not only is he working, but he's trying to be more discreet about it, as you suggested.'

The superintendent shrugged his shoulders grumpily.

'Let's go to bed,' continued M. Allou. 'I'm ready to drop. Tomorrow he'll bring us his report.'

'I'm not going to lose any sleep over it,' growled Sallent.

Chapter XIII

M. ALLOU'S PROMISE

At eight o'clock the following morning, Proto asked to see the superintendent, who was coming down the stairs with M. Allou.

'Nothing to report before midnight,' he announced.

'And afterwards?'

'Afterwards it was my colleague. He couldn't have seen anything, because otherwise he would have phoned in a report.'

'So nothing unusual happened last night?'

'Absolutely nothing.'

At that moment the concierge approached.

'There's a call for *M. le Commissaire* from M. Clermon.'

Sallent reached the phone booth in three strides. Proto stood there, scratching his head in embarrassment.

'My God,' he said to M. Allou, 'if something did happen, I'm toast. But I swear I was there this time.'

The superintendent was already talking:

'Hello, M. Clermon?'

'Yes.'

'Nothing serious, I hope?'

'No, just something annoying. I wouldn't have bothered you but for your adventure last night, which the inspector told me about.'

'You saw him?'

'Naturally, when he brought poor Madras back.'

'Ah, yes. How is he?'

'Not too bad. He'll be fully recovered after a few days' rest. But he had a narrow escape.'

'To say the least. Well, that's good to hear. What happened to you?'

'Someone stole one of my cars. The one you saw yesterday, in fact.'

'Where was it parked?'

'In the garage at the back of the house.'

'At what time?'

'That I couldn't say.'

'And you suspect Allevaire, naturally.'

'Of course. If he was trying to escape....'

'Did he know how to drive?'

'Very well. And, furthermore, he knew the vehicle well because I'd lent it to him often.'

'Who had keys to the garage? Hello? Hello? How annoying, the line's gone dead. Hello?'

'Hello?'

'We were cut off. I was asking who had keys to the garage?'

'Only me. It's on my key chain. But it's a simple lock, very easy to pick.'

'Very well. Give me the number of the vehicle and a brief description, and I'll alert everyone.'

Sallent took down the information and left the cabin. He found M. Allou at the main entrance.

'Would you believe, Dupont....'

'I gathered from your replies that someone has stolen one of Clermon's cars?'

'Yes. That's not surprising if Allevaire—.'

'There is something surprising, however.'

'What?'

'That your conversation was disconnected and re-established. That never happens with automatic service.'

'That's true. I wasn't paying attention.'

'Do you recall what you were discussing at that moment?'

'Wait... It was concerning the key to the garage.'

'You had to wait a long time for a response.'

'True enough.'

Proto approached the two men.

'What's happening?' he asked.

His very presence was enough to infuriate Sallent.

'You! You again! Needless to say, when you were on duty, someone stole a car.'

'But... where was the garage?'

'Behind.'

'But how could I have... Besides, I spent a long time in hospital with the wounded man.'

Sallent shrugged his shoulders and walked away. M. Allou couldn't help smiling. Proto approached him:

'It's not fair! I don't know why he can't stand the sight of me.'

'Not at all,' replied M. Allou. 'He has his moments, like all of us. But, deep down, he respects you.'

'Do you really think so?'

'I'm sure of it. And to prove it, he's asked me to charge you with a delicate mission.'

'That's marvellous. What is it?'

'Wait. Take a look. Do you know this man?'

M. Allou had taken out the driving licence in the name of Pierre Fumage, which had been found in Allevaire's wallet.

Proto studied the photograph.

'No,' he said. 'The superintendent's going to criticise me again, even though this fellow came from Grenoble!'

'Don't get upset. We need to know if Fumage ever came to Bordeaux, whether he met Allevaire and Le Borgne and, if so, what was their relationship?'

'That's not going to be easy,' replied Proto, scratching his head.

'You have nothing else to do today, because Madras is in bed. Check the usual police informers: someone amongst them may recognise the fellow. Tonight, when you come to make your report, I'll give you further information, which I'll have obtained from Grenoble in the meantime. Good luck.'

***

After Proto had left, M. Allou went over to Sallent, who was reading the newspaper in a corner of the room.

'You would do well to telephone the examining magistrate to ask him to telegraph a request for more information about Fumage. He knows your voice, so I can't do it.'

'I'll do it straight away.'

After the superintendent returned from the phone booth, he found M. Allou smoking his pipe, eyes half-closed.

'What are you thinking about?' he asked.

'Something that Clermon said yesterday morning. A theory he put forward to excuse his future brother-in-law from his slanderous statement.'

'Remind me.'

'That Madras had possibly been less heroic than he claimed on the

95

night of the intrusion, when Allevaire attempted his first theft.'

'Ah, yes, I remember, replied Sallent. 'Clermon insinuated that his secretary might not have tried to subdue the man, but had merely chased him, leaving the possibility that he'd made an error about the man's identity.'

'Precisely. It had seemed quite plausible at the time. But last night Madras showed himself to be very courageous.'

'That's true.'

'Which means we need to revisit the theory of the slanderous accusation. Physical courage is sometimes accompanied by moral cowardice. Do you remember his determination to marry the young woman, despite her tears?'

'Yes,' said Sallent.

He sat down beside M. Allou and, after a moment, asked:

'What are we going to do today?'

'Not much. Await the information I requested.'

'Sounds like fun.'

M. Allou paused and then smiled:

'If you want to amuse yourself, my dear Sallent, you could try a small experiment.'

'Such as?'

'If it doesn't work out, it'll at least stop you grumbling for a few minutes, which would be a miracle in itself. Telephone the local police station for R... Street.'

'To ask what?'

'If by any chance they patrolled the street behind Clermon's townhouse during the course of last night.'

'What do you want to verify... Dupont?'

'The telephone line cut-off.'

'Are you serious?'

'Yes. Just do it.'

'And supposing there was a patrol?'

'Send them here.'

A few minutes later, Sallent returned.

'There was a patrol, which went past at around two o'clock in the morning. They'll be here in a few minutes.'

***

96

The two men soon arrived.

'Do you know M. Clermon's garage?' asked M. Allou.

'Yes.'

'Did you notice anything unusual last night?'

'Yes. Not much, though. M. Clermon had forgotten his door key.'

'That's all. Thank you very much. Oh, just one more thing. Do you know the cars he keeps there?'

'Yes, of course. A two-seater and a larger vehicle which can take six.'

'Who drives them?'

'The chauffeur, before he left a month ago. After that, it was mostly M. Clermon and occasionally his sister. I don't believe M. Madras knows how to drive.'

'Perfect, gentlemen.'

After the police had left, M. Allou turned to Sallent with a smile:

'There!' he said. 'It looks as though there were two keys.'

'Obviously! But was the other lent out by Marthe Clermon?'

'Indeed it was. And that explains the line being cut off and the delayed response. I'm being kind, my dear Sallent: I've given you the opportunity of revenge against the young lady.'

'And what use is the information?'

'None, because you're still grumbling.'

Sallent shrugged his shoulders, then replied in his most soothing voice:

'Given that nothing must be done to inconvenience her in any way, or ask her the most inoffensive question, what she may have done is of no importance.'

'That's not fair, Sallent. We were on our way to interview her last night. It's not my fault that events took an unexpected turn. We can go back this morning, if you like.'

'Oh, it's not really important. All she did was help Allevaire because she's in love with him. How could that possibly matter?'

'So you'd leave me to interview her by myself, Sallent? Because I do intend to talk to her.'

'Because you have time to spare. Speaking of spare, what are we doing in Bordeaux? We came here because you suspected collusion between Madras and Allevaire. Now that you've abandoned that idea, and our suspect is on the run....'

'I still believe that the nub of the problem is here. Le Borgne interests me. He must know something and may even be part of the gang. If we shadow him successfully, he could lead us to something important. I've a hunch our adventure has just begun.'

'May heaven be your witness. Personally, I think we're just treading water.'

***

At around eleven o'clock, M. Allou arrived at the Clermon residence and asked to see his sister.

When he saw her come in, so slight with large eyes full of sadness and fear, he felt pity for her once again. The child must not be sacrificed, neither to her brother, nor to a villain.

'Please sit down,' he said. 'I'm not here as an enemy, I assure you, nor even to interrogate you. I already know everything I need to know about you.'

She looked down and said nothing.

'The authorities will not be told anything, because they have no need to know. It doesn't matter to them that, the day before yesterday, you opened the door to Allevaire who, when discovered by M. Clermon, was thrown out with justifiable brutality. It doesn't matter to them that yesterday you warned him of our impending departure to his hiding place. And that afterwards you lent him your garage key in order to take the car.'

She didn't move a muscle except at the tip of her chin, which trembled slightly.

'Do you acknowledge all that, miss?'

She nodded very slightly in agreement.

'My child, nobody can reproach you for having been seduced by the charms of that man. Many others, with far more experience, have succumbed. But now, you should understand. You know what he is. No longer is there a deceitful halo hiding the true nature of the villain. He's just a cheap little crook with no redeeming features. He has none of the inner feelings which even the most hardened criminals possess. His last offence was particularly shameful: stealing from his old aunt, who had always been so good to him. And stealing what was dearest to her heart, a set of silverware which wasn't even of any great value. It was a despicable act, don't you agree?'

'Yes,' murmured Marthe.

'Think about it, my child. And think about another risk you may be running. During that first night when a man broke in here—whilst Allevaire was committing that despicable crime in Limonest—he passed right in front of your room whilst he was running away. It's impossible for you not to have known for certain that it wasn't Allevaire. A woman has no doubts when it comes to the person she loves. So why did you lie? Why did you say you couldn't be sure?'

Marthe's chin started to tremble and there were now tears in her eyes.

'Is it because you were afraid of contradicting Serge Madras?' continued M. Allou.

'N-No, it wasn't that,' she stammered.

'No? Obviously you dared not admit it. Now tell me: do you want to marry Serge?'

'No, I don't....'

Her voice was so low that M. Allou had to lean forward to hear it.

'But your brother insists, doesn't he?'

'Yes, sir. Oh, if you could only....'

'Only what?'

'I trust you. Just don't tell him you heard it from me. If you could only persuade my brother to abandon the project... But please, please, don't tell him you've spoken to me.'

'How frightened you seem to be. Shouldn't you be telling me everything?

'There's nothing else to tell! I don't love Serge, that's all.'

'I'll try and convince your brother, as soon as I have an opportunity.'

'Please hurry.'

'Why?'

'The engagement will be officially announced tomorrow. I don't want it to happen!'

'I'll be seeing your brother tonight. But Serge Madras isn't much of a man to insist on marrying in such circumstances.'

'Oh, sir, don't speak ill of him. That wouldn't be fair. He doesn't know.'

'You've disguised your feelings?'

'Yes. I was about to tell him when Gustave Allevaire was exposed. After that, I didn't dare any more. But he loves me sincerely. And he thinks the feeling is returned.'

'In that case, make it clear to him.'

'No! Never! He would understand everything.'

'Understand what?'

'Everything you've described. My rendezvous on the night before last, when I opened the door, and the help I gave Allevaire yesterday. He has such an admiration for me... I don't want him to know.'

'Very well, I promise you he won't. I'll only speak to your brother. I'll come and see him after dinner. You can count on me.'

'Don't tell him you've seen me.'

'Agreed. Are you so afraid of your brother, then?'

'It's not that. On the contrary, he's always been so good to me... He brought me up after the deaths of our parents. And in the beginning we weren't rich. He gave up everything for me. That's why I don't want to hurt him by refusing the marriage he desires so much. But I don't want him to know that I've confided in a stranger... What will you tell him?'

'I don't know yet... But I'll find a way, trust me. And now you must stop crying.'

Chapter XIV

AN ABRUPT DEPARTURE

M. Allou joined Sallent for lunch.

'What's new?'

'Nothing, Dupont. And you?'

'Nothing either.'

'Come on, admit it. I can see it in your face. It was her, wasn't it? You can say so, I don't care. I'm only asking you so I don't go off on a wild goose chase.'

'Yes, it was she... But promise never to tell anyone, Sallent!'

'I promise. Apart from that, nothing interesting to report?'

'No, but this afternoon we should get some news. Don't leave the hotel.'

***

The first telephone call came at three o'clock. The superintendent was informed that Le Borgne's movements had given no cause for suspicion. He even seemed to be more energetic than before and had visited numerous clients with an unaccustomed zeal.

'Perfect,' said Sallent as he joined M. Allou again. 'He's trying to allay suspicion. I assume he's up to something fishy.'

'And, furthermore, his approach is excellent. Visiting a great many people is the best way to disguise seeing the two or three persons you actually need to see.'

'Obviously.'

A courier from the *Palais de Justice* arrived just before five o'clock.

'There's a letter for you from the examining magistrate, superintendent.'

'Thank you. Give it to me.'

As soon as the man had left, Sallent handed the envelope to M. Allou.

'No, no,' said the other. 'Open it yourself. I'm Dupont, your subordinate. Practice treating me with no respect. It's the prudent

101

thing to do, and I detest respect anyway.'

Sallent opened the envelope. It contained an official telegram from Grenoble:

"Fumage travelling salesman. Bachelor. Works regularly. Enquiries positive. Often away, left eight days ago."

'That's a fat lot of help,' said the superintendent. 'They don't even know he's dead!'

'What did you expect? Stop complaining, your friend's here.'

It was indeed Proto who was coming towards them at a rapid pace. His squat, stocky body quivered as a smile revealed his enormous teeth.

'Superintendent, sir,' he exclaimed joyfully. 'This time you're going to be proud of me!'

'Hmm,' grunted Sallent.

'I've successfully completed the mission you charged me with.'

'Charged you with mission? Must've been drunk.'

'I transmitted your wishes this morning,' intervened M. Allou hastily. 'You remember... whatever he could find about Fumage.'

'Ah, yes. Perfect. Found out he was travelling salesman, did you?'

'You knew already?' said Proto with an air of disappointment. 'But there's more.'

'Let's hear it.'

'He came here frequently to sell lace.'

'Really? Lace? Fascinating.'

'Let me finish. One day, in one of the cafés, he met Allevaire. They appeared to know each other, because they were friendly and talked in hushed voices. No one knows what they said, but suddenly there was a violent eruption. "I'll do what I want," shouted Fumage. "You'll pay, and more dearly than you think!" replied Allevaire. There were more words, equally violent, but in a lower voice again. Then one of them finished by announcing: "I'll settle your account once and for all. We'll meet again."'

'That's not bad,' admitted Sallent, grudgingly. 'You're making progress. Anything else to report? His reputation?'

'Excellent. He was seen as a very reputable salesman.'

'And when did this dispute take place?'

'They couldn't tell me exactly, but it was about six days ago. It's now the fourteenth, so around the seventh or eighth of May.'

'Good. My compliments. You may go.'

102

'You could have been more friendly towards him,' laughed M. Allou after Proto had left. 'He did a good job, the poor fellow.'

'Yes... if I could be sure he was telling the truth.'

'Why would he lie?'

'Oh, not with malicious intent. Simply to make you believe he was working: he invents everything.'

'No, Sallent, you're not being fair. He's lazy, certainly, but that doesn't make him a liar. On the contrary, what he reported sounds plausible. Fumage's "account" was indeed settled, on the night of the ninth of May. Not by Allevaire, obviously, but he was certainly aware of it, which helps my theory enormously. He counted on the murder to establish an alibi and to be reborn as someone with an excellent reputation.'

'All very convenient,' retorted Sallent, 'but Proto could equally have made up his story to coincide with events. Fumage dies on the ninth, so he invents a dispute two days earlier.'

'No, he didn't know that Fumage had been murdered.'

'You didn't tell him?'

'Of course not. He knew nothing at all about the man.'

'Couldn't he have recognised him from newspaper photographs?'

'There weren't any. I forbade it.'

'Well, in that case... what Proto said must be correct.'

'You seem annoyed about it, Sallent. You mustn't be so unfair.'

'You're right. What do you want me to say? He irritates me. But he's no worse than many others, after all. There are good cops and bad cops, just as in everything else.'

'Just as in everything else,' agreed M. Allou ruefully.

***

They dined together. Sallent was morose.

'What's wrong?'

'I'm bored. Nothing's happening.'

'The fact is,' said M. Allou, 'that this case lacks mystery. I want a puzzle... something improbable, impossible... something which makes me rack my brains and forces me to apply my powers of logic. This one puts me to sleep.'

'Me, too. I think I'll go to bed.'

'I have a visit to make first.'

'To Clermon?' asked the superintendent, with a wicked smile.

103

'Again? Sometimes you question that young woman too much, and sometimes not enough.'

'You're wrong. It's her brother I'm going to see.'

'About what?'

'About her marriage.'

'Well, you must have time on your hands. Either that, or you're going to ask her hand for yourself.'

'Not yet, not yet. I wish you a pleasant night, my dear superintendent.'

'I expect it to be peaceful.'

***

The magistrate was immediately ushered into Clermon's office.

The mission was going to be delicate. M. Allou looked at his adversary, the eyes alert in his young, thin face. The man wasn't an idiot, and prudence would be needed if he were not to suspect something.

'You put forward a theory the other day,' he began,

'About what?'

'About the encounter between Serge Madras and the man he took to be Allevaire.'

'Yes, I remember. I told you my secretary had possibly acted less courageously than he'd claimed and had not, in fact, tackled the man, but only seen him from behind as he was running away. And in that way, an error may have occurred, but not deliberately.'

'That's it. Do you still think so?'

'Yes. Why shouldn't I?'

'Even after the events of last night? I saw Madras with my own eyes, pursuing the miscreant and trying to stop him, all alone. I can attest to his courage, and courageous people don't usually boast.'

'You have a point,' agreed Clermon.

'Yes, but do you see the consequence?'

'Go on.'

'You already know it,' continued M. Allou. 'Unless Madras was genuinely mistaken, he made a slanderous accusation. And, I have to tell you, that seems to be the general opinion.'

'So?'

'So, I thought it was my duty to tell you. You spoke to me the other day of an impending marriage.'

104

'Thank you,' replied Clermon curtly, 'for your interest in my personal affairs. The police's concern is very touching.'

M. Allou fought back his anger. Under normal circumstances, he would not have tolerated being spoken to like that. But he had a mission to accomplish, and all self-respect would have to be sacrificed.

'I thought it was the right thing to do,' he replied. 'I couldn't have imagined you to be so indifferent about your sister's future that you would allow her to marry a man so tainted that he will probably be arrested in the near future for giving false evidence.'

Clermon had already risen from his chair.

'My sister is quite old enough to make her own decisions,' he declared. 'And, because she loves the young man, I haven't the right to oppose what she believes to be her happiness. I demand the same discretion from strangers.'

M. Allou bit his lip. He fought with all his might to avoid hurling the word "Liar" in the man's face. Alas, he'd made a promise and was obliged to appear credulous.

'Very well,' he said. 'The event will take place in prison. It will certainly be the talk of the town.'

Clermon was about to reply when the door bell rang.

'Who could it be at this hour?' he murmured.

Voices could be heard below:

'Wait, gentlemen, whom should I announce?'

'Out of the way. We don't need anyone.'

Footsteps sounded on the stairs. Without knocking, Sallent came into the room.

M. Allou, already taken by surprise by the intrusion, was even more so when he noticed the wide silhouette of Proto behind the tall one of the superintendent. What extraordinary circumstance could have brought these two men together?

But Proto, with his strident voice and magnificent accent, was already shouting explanations.

'An event, Dupont. Le Borgne has flown the coop!'

'He's gone?'

'Come along,' said Sallent. 'We'll explain.'

But his voice couldn't be heard above the inspector's, who continued:

'He took a train at six o'clock. Luckily, a colleague of mine was following him. He only went fifty kilometres and got out at Landornerie, with my colleague still behind him. He's a crafty one, he is. There's no one to match him for shadowing, not even in Paris. He followed our man out into the country and saw him go into an isolated house. Then he ran to phone us and is waiting back at the hotel. I think this time we've got Allevaire!'

He had been talking so exuberantly it would have been impossible to stop him.

'You talk too much,' snarled Sallent, giving him a furious look.

'What time is the next train?' asked M. Allou.

'Tomorrow at seven o'clock. It's a small local line.'

'Does the *Sûreté* have a car?'

'Yes, but it's broken down.'

Clermon stepped forward and said, in a quiet voice:

'I can drive you there, gentlemen. I have a car that's big enough.'

'You're too kind.'

'It's normal. A taxi would take you two hours on that bumpy road. We'll be there in fifty minutes.'

'I accept,' said M. Allou. 'We have to move fast.'

'I only have one condition, gentlemen. Apart from driving you there, I don't want to be involved in any way.'

'Of course not,' said the superintendent. 'It's not your job. It'll be dangerous.'

'Oh, it's not that, believe me. I'm happy to help you with this arrest, which I wholeheartedly wish for. But I have my own reasons for demanding that my own role be kept absolutely quiet. Absolutely, do you hear? And that includes keeping it from the villain as well.'

'I understand,' replied M. Allou. 'We won't talk about it anywhere, even in your own home.'

'Who are we going to bring?' asked Sallent. 'There are only two of us for the arrest.'

'Excuse me, three,' said Proto.

'Ah, yes, I was forgetting. But if you're too tired....'

'Excuse me, superintendent, sir,' declared the inspector loudly. 'I've been assigned to the case and I'm not going to have the Paris police take it from under my nose. If there's to be an arrest, I have the right to be involved.'

'As you wish. That still only leaves—.'

'Three!' announced Proto.

106

'Four,' said M. Allou, 'because we're going to meet up with the inspector who alerted us.'

'That's right,' said Sallent. 'And it appears he's very good.'

'And, furthermore,' continued M. Allou, 'it would be ridiculous to add more for the arrest of one man.'

'Agreed. Let's go.'

'Follow me,' said Clermon. 'Let's not make too much noise, so as not to make my sister anxious. Her room is next door. The car is in the garage and, as luck would have it, has a full tank.'

'Let's hope the tyres haven't been slashed,' murmured Sallent in M. Allou's ear. 'With that imbecile braying like an ass just now....'

'In any case,' replied M. Allou, 'in remote places like the one we're going to, the telephone stops working after nine o'clock, and it's already twenty to ten. That's already a bit of luck. So stop grousing!'

They reached the garage. The tyres were intact and the car started right away.

Chapter XV

THE INCREDIBLE ADVENTURE

They drove fast through the night with no one saying a word. They traversed several villages already asleep and finally, just before eleven o'clock, arrived in Landornerie.

They stopped in front of the hotel *Golden Sun* and asked the owner if M. Léglise was there; that was the name of the inspector.

'Yes, gentlemen, certainly. He awaits you in his bed.'

'In his bed?'

'The poor devil fell down the stairs a short while ago. He's sprained a leg. The doctor's examined him. It's not serious: he'll be up and about in a week.'

'Thank you,' growled Sallent. 'A week... Well, at least we can talk to him.'

They went up to his room and Léglise told them what little he knew. Etrillat had got off at the station, reached the open country, and headed in the direction of a remotely situated house.

'Did he go in?'

'I didn't see. If I'd tried to follow him in the open fields, he would soon have noticed me. I preferred to call you urgently.'

'That was the right thing to do.'

'I'm sorry I won't be able to come with you. You won't have any difficulty finding the house; you can't miss it.'

In fact, his directions, together with a drawing, made everything perfectly clear.

'We can't afford to lose a minute,' said Sallent. 'It's at least three kilometres away, if I've understood correctly.'

'Roughly. But if you have a car, you can get to within a hundred metres with your lights out.'

'As close as that?'

'Yes, the house is in a depression and can't monitor traffic coming from the right. That's the route you have to take.'

They left.

One kilometre before their destination, Clermon extinguished the

109

lights.

'Good heavens, I hadn't realised how dark the sky was. I think it's about to rain... That'll make it difficult to drive. If we go really slowly we'll make less noise and be sure not to lose our way.'

Besides, Léglise had been right, there was no possibility of error. They reached the crest of a hill, from which the house was clearly visible. But, as they descended, it was again hidden from view.

'We should stop here,' said Sallent. 'I recognise the marker he described to us.'

Clermon drove into a field and hid the car in a cluster of trees. They all got out.

'Follow me,' said Sallent. 'Nobody make a noise. And if I have the misfortune to hear you, M. Proto....'

'I'm just as careful as anyone else.'

The little group advanced in total silence and soon arrived beneath the walls of the huge house. Just as Clermon had predicted, it started to rain, which made everything even darker.

They worked their way slowly around the building. All the shutters were closed and there were no lights to be seen anywhere. The superintendent placed M. Allou at one corner of the house facing the rear façade, and Proto at the other corner.

'I'm going to ring the door bell,' he said in a murmur. 'If he tries to get out through a window, arrest him. If he opens the door, I'll take care of him.'

'I'm going to distance myself,' said Clermon. 'As I told you, I don't want to be involved. When you arrest him, take him on foot to the village and don't talk about my car.'

'Understood.'

Clermon disappeared into the darkness and Sallent went to the front door, where he tugged at a cord hanging to the side. The sound of a bell resonated for a long time.

The superintendent waited for a full minute and rang again. Inside the house nothing moved.

'I'm going to have to go in, after all,' murmured Sallent.

He took a bunch of picklocks out of his pocket.

Suddenly someone touched his arm and he sprang back.

'It's me,' said M. Allou. 'Proto's enough to guard the rear.'

'I'd prefer—.'

'It's not about your preferences. You are not going into this house alone! An ambush would be only too easy. If the fellow escapes from the rear, that's too bad.'

'If you were under my orders,' growled Sallent, 'I'd send you back to your post smartly.'

'Maybe, but that's not the case. Try to open the door.'

The superintendent inserted one of the picklocks, manipulated it for a few seconds and smiled in satisfaction: the latch moved.

'Let's hope it's not bolted,' he murmured.

The door opened and, luckily, didn't creak. The two men entered.

The darkness was total and there was no possibility of making out any shapes. They stood where they were and concentrated hard. Not a sound could be heard.

The superintendent switched on his electric torch and swept the beam around the room.

They were in a vestibule, from which led three doors, currently shut: one to the left, one to the right, and another to the rear, next to the foot of the stairs.

They opened the left abruptly and saw a dining room sparsely furnished: a table, a few chairs, and a small sideboard. Nobody could hide in there.

Next was a salon with a couple of rustic sofas and nowhere to hide.

Finally, to the rear, was the kitchen, equally bare.

Each time, they took a few steps into the room to make sure the shutters were indeed properly fastened from the inside by hooks.

'There are still two floors above us,' whispered the superintendent. 'Luckily they all follow the same plan. With every room opening onto a central vestibule, there's no chance of anyone escaping without being seen during our visit.'

They went up to the first floor, which was, as the superintendent had said, laid out in the same fashion. Whilst one man went in to a room the other stood in the doorway, making any to-and-fro impossible.

The work was harder because the rooms were fully furnished with beds and wardrobes which had to be examined.

One of the rooms had recently been inhabited: there was a smell of tobacco and the bed sheets had been slightly disturbed.

It was the only interesting clue they discovered. Everywhere, the shutters were firmly secured.

On the second floor and the attic, the inspection proved equally

111

fruitless.

'We're going to have to look at the roof,' said Sallent.

'That won't be necessary. Look, the skylight is padlocked.'

The superintendent, ever suspicious, shook the padlock vigorously.

'You're right, he couldn't have got up there. Someone's been making fun of us.'

'Not necessarily. Allevaire needs to eat; he may well have an accomplice in the village, but he daren't go there in the daylight. He could well have left and will return later.'

'That's true. We can wait for him in the house.'

'Not prudent.'

'Well, that's a surprise, coming from you.'

'You don't understand. We might wait in vain. He's a wily fox, as you know. He could have placed some kind of marker on the door and will know immediately he arrives that someone has opened it. Then, obviously, he won't come in.'

'Dammit, you're right. We'll have to lie in wait outside. On the way down, we'll need to check again, just to be sure. Suppose he came back while we were upstairs?'

'With the door he'd have found open? Hardly likely. It's best to get out of here as soon as possible.'

'You never know. Hiding somewhere that's already been searched isn't all that stupid. He might think it the safest place to be. And it's quickly done.'

They'd been careful not to close the cupboard doors or move back any displaced furniture, so the inspection was rapid: it was enough to give a glance from the doorway—and, obviously, look behind the door and under the bed if need be.

The house was just as empty as it had been before. That was absolutely certain.

'You see,' said Sallent. 'It only took five minutes and our conscience is clear.'

They found themselves once again outside. The superintendent was careful to close the front door. In fact, he only needed to pull it, and it locked itself automatically.

'That's not necessary,' observed M. Allou.

'It's a matter of principle. Always leave things as you found them. Hell's bells, the rain's getting heavier. I should have brought a coat.'

'Me too. But it was so hot when we left.'

The superintendent gave a low whistle. The signal was enough for Proto, who appeared a few moments later.

'Did you see anything?' asked Sallent.

'Nothing at all. And you?'

'Nothing either. There's no point in you staying at the rear of the house. He can't get in through any of the windows, because all the shutters are locked.'

Clermon appeared and approached the group.

'He wasn't inside?' he asked.

'No, but we're hoping he comes back.'

'Are you going to wait?'

'All night, if necessary.'

'Well, I'll leave you to it. It's raining too hard. I'm going back to my car to sleep a little. You can join me later if you're empty-handed. But you're going to catch your death of cold…'

'The job's the job,' replied Sallent.

'True. By the way, there's a small tool shed which I discovered ten metres from here, under the trees on this side. Goodnight.'

'Goodnight.'

Clermon left. The rain came down even harder.

'Bloody weather,' grumbled the superintendent.

'It's all the same to me,' said Proto.

Sallent touched him with his hand, for he was scarcely visible.

'You've a leather coat, for heaven's sake. Very clever.'

'Are you reproaching me again?'

'Be quiet. We mustn't talk. Let's move away from the door. Five metres. They won't see us. And silence!'

But he immediately set a bad example, leaning over towards M. Allou.

'I'm shivering. How about you?'

'The same.'

'You're going to catch pneumonia. Go to that shed.'

'No, Sallent, I'm staying with you.'

'That's silly. Why? Seven metres more and you'd still get to the man at the same time as us.'

'I'd be afraid all alone.'

Sallent shrugged his shoulders.

'That's silly,' he repeated. 'There's no reason for you to get wet, just because I do. How does it help if we both get soaked?'

'What you say makes sense, Sallent. So, go to the shed. That way, we won't both get soaked.'

'I'm used to it.'

'And I'm used to sharing my companion's lot.'

'No offence, but you're as stubborn as a mule. So be it, I'll go to the shed. After all, ten metres isn't far. I can react swiftly. Are you coming with me?'

'Yes. On second thoughts, the distance won't count for much. And Proto can signal the man's arrival.'

'He can stay outside,' grunted Sallent. 'He's got a leather coat, after all.'

He went over to the inspector, standing on the other side of the door.

'We'll be in the little shed,' he informed him. 'Don't be afraid, we'll only be ten metres away.'

'I'm not afraid!'

'Very well. We won't be able to see Allevaire when he reaches the door. Don't wait for him to try and open it, just switch on your torch, that'll be the signal. We can be there in a few seconds. And if he tries to run away… too bad, I'll fire. He did the same thing last night.'

'Right, superintendent, sir.'

'Can you be sure to pick him out in the dark? I'll stand by the door and you tell me if you can see me. I'm wearing dark clothes, so that'll be a good test.'

'I can distinguish you perfectly clearly,' said Proto.

'So any distraction would be inexcusable, is that clear?'

'Perfectly. You can count on me. By the way, in case of danger… may I fire as well?'

'Yes, but not out of panic. Goodnight.'

And Sallent disappeared into the night.

***

A few minutes later, M. Allou and the superintendent were in the tool shed.

'It's certainly better here,' said Sallent.

'Yes, but poor Proto out there alone must be scared stiff.'

'That's too bad. He shouldn't have brought a coat. But quiet! Can I hear someone walking?'

'You're dreaming, my poor Sallent. It's only water dripping from

114

the branches.'

'So it is. But it's best we don't talk, in any case.'

M. Allou leant back against one side of the shed and tried to take a nap. But, after a quarter of an hour, he felt Sallent tug on his arm and heard him murmur:

'Look.'

'Where?'

'The house.'

'I can't see anything.'

'On the first floor.'

M. Allou stared hard, but could see nothing.

'Wait… There! Did you see that?'

There had indeed been a brief flicker of light behind one of the shutters.

'That's the third time,' continued the superintendent. 'There's someone in the house. In the room with the sheets on the bed.'

'Right. What's happening?'

'Not hard to guess. He's collecting his stuff before skipping out.'

'Who?'

'Allevaire, for heaven's sake!'

'How did he get in?'

'Through the door. Proto must have gone off to hide somewhere. Come along. We'll take a look. Quietly!'

They advanced on tiptoe. Thanks to the wet ground they were able to walk in absolute silence. (And, in any case, the rain was falling so heavily it would have masked even a fairly loud noise.)

As they approached, Sallent was able to make out a silhouette against the house wall. So Proto was indeed at his post. But was he watching seriously?

He certainly was, for the superintendent was still some way from the door when he found himself bathed in a beam of light. It lasted only a moment as Proto recognised him immediately.

'What's happening, superintendent, sir?'

'You've let someone get in!'

'I assure you I haven't. I would have seen him, just as I saw you. There's nobody, I swear. Unless they got in at the back.'

'Impossible, the shutters are firmly secured. We'll see.'

Once again the superintendent used the picklock to open the door without the slightest noise. Proto and M. Allou slid in behind him.

Silently they climbed the stairs and arrived in front of the door of the room where the light had shone. Sallent tried to peer through the keyhole, but realised that the key from the other side blocked it completely. So, in one swift movement, he opened the door and switched on his torch.

Someone was there but, unfortunately, too close. Before the commissionaire had the chance to see him, the man brought a hard object down on his hand. The torch fell to the floor and went out.

Sallent lunged in the direction of the blow, but although his hand brushed against some clothing, he was unable to grab hold of it.

As soon as the door had opened, M. Allou and Proto had rushed into the room with their torches lit. Too late! The beams, badly directed at first, could only catch a form disappearing through the wall to their left, where there was a communicating door to the adjacent room.

M. Allou rushed towards it, assuming that Proto or Sallent would go to the vestibule and cut off the man's escape.

Unfortunately, Sallent was at that moment facing the wall to the right and hadn't seen anything. He only understood what had happened when M. Allou reached the other room. It was too late; the fugitive had already reached the landing.

Sallent leapt towards the sound of the closing door. Without a light, he could only listen to someone racing down the stairs. He threw himself after them; luckily M. Allou joined him and shone his torch downwards.

But, halfway down, the staircase turned, and the man was already outside the beam of light.

The two men descended until their torches illuminated the downstairs vestibule. At the far end a man was running, framed by the front door, which was partly open.

Sallent fired. But at the last instant, he must have had scruples about shooting an unarmed man in the back, for the shot went high.

At the sound of the report, the fugitive instinctively turned and the light fully illuminated his face. It was undoubtedly Allevaire!

But, at the same time, he slid behind the half-open door into the night. When the three men—for Proto had now joined them—reached the garden, nobody could be seen.

Chapter XVI

RIDDLES

There was no point in contemplating pursuit in the dense, bushy garden; Allevaire knew all the paths, whereas the three men could distinguish nothing in the total darkness. And the fugitive's footsteps would be covered by the rain pattering in the branches.

'Well, that's that,' said Sallent. 'But now for the explanations.'

He went back inside and closed the door.

He found an oil lamp in the salon and lit it.

'Come in, gentlemen,' he called out.

M. Allou and Proto joined him.

'Sit down, M. Proto. Let's not waste any time. Can you tell me what just happened?'

'I can only think of one explanation, chief: the man got in through one of the windows.'

'Impossible. All the shutters were bolted when we first visited the house.'

'Apparently, at least, superintendent, sir. Perhaps one of the hooks wasn't properly embedded in the wall, so that the shutter could simply be pushed in from the outside?'

'Very well, let's examine that theory immediately.'

Sallent's icy tone was more disquieting than any angry outburst.

'Let's examine the shutters,' he continued. 'Starting with this room.'

He flung wide all the windows.

'But come closer, M. Proto, I beg you. Look for yourself. Does this hook look loosely embedded to you?'

And the superintendent shook it with all his force.

'Try it yourself. Does it move? No? Try the next one. Still no? Maybe the next. Shake it, shake it!'

And the superintendent, expressionless, dragged Proto from room to room, repeating the same procedure each time.

'Everything secure, Proto? Are you sure? Let's go up to the first floor.'

'Oh, that won't be necessary.'

'But yes. He could have used a ladder. We have to check everything.'

At each floor, the result was the same. They went back downstairs and the superintendent sat down again.

'So, M. Proto, your theory was not correct. The only way in was though the door. Do you see any other solution?'

'Yes. There was a hiding place or a secret passage, maybe a cave?'

'Perfect. Look for them, M. Proto, look for them. Take your time. There's wood in the fireplace, I'm going to light a fire so that I can dry out.'

For over an hour, they could hear the inspector banging on the walls and partitions with his huge fists.

Eventually he reappeared in the salon.

'No,' he said. 'There's nothing to be found.'

'Well, well. Another theory to be rejected.'

'Did you check everything, chief? The beds, the wardrobes?'

'Rest assured, my lad. Twice, even. Once going up and once coming down. I even thought about the roof. There was nobody in the house when we left. But afterwards, there was someone. Do we agree on that?'

'Obviously. I've seen with my own eyes.'

'So, can you tell me how he got in?'

'I give up.'

'But you do agree it must have been through the door?'

'Listen, chief. It appears to be obvious yet, at the same time, impossible.'

'Obvious, yes, but why impossible?'

'Because I would have seen him.'

'There's the whole question, M. Proto.'

The inspector stood up and declared in an indignant voice:

'Chief, I won't permit anyone to doubt me, not even you. In any case, you know I was at my post: I saw you when you appeared.'

'Yes, you were there then.'

'I didn't move one centimetre!'

M. Allou intervened.

'Listen, old chap, anyone can be negligent for a moment, even me. But we keep it between ourselves, after a good dressing-down by the boss. But the superintendent is no snitch, I can assure you. He may say a few harsh things, but he won't repeat them in Bordeaux. Isn't that right, superintendent?'

'I promise,' grunted Sallent, who obeyed M. Allou without question.

'You see? Because he's not your usual boss, there'll be no record of this. But things will go very badly for you if our investigation goes astray because you persisted in hiding the truth. Do you understand?'

'Superintendent, sir,' said Proto, 'I trust what you said. If I had committed an error, I would have told you. But I swear I wasn't distracted for a single moment. On the contrary, I wanted to rehabilitate myself in your eyes and at the same time those of the Bordeaux police, which I'm honoured to belong to. So I watched very diligently. I hoped to arrest the man myself. He never came near the door.'

'Very well, let's get out of here. Our clothes are dry and there's nothing more to be done.'

Outside the rain had stopped. They set off in the direction of the car.

The superintendent let Proto lead the way and murmured in M. Allou's ear:

'I wouldn't want to accuse you lightly,' he said, 'but am I right in thinking you believed his protests?'

'Let's not exaggerate. I'm not sure that Proto abandoned his post, and I'm not sure that he didn't.'

'If he was telling the truth, then we're all mad!' exclaimed Sallent.

'Maybe… But that's a solution I'll only admit as a last resort.'

'Can you think of another one?'

'My dear Sallent, riddles are there to be solved, not denied.'

'You love them so much,' growled the other, 'that you imagine them purely for the pleasure. As for me, it's obvious that Proto was distracted and left his post.'

'I don't believe it. He would have feared being double-checked, which is exactly what happened. We were too close by for him to allow himself a fantasy; at least he would have waited longer: as it is, we hadn't been in the shed for more than a quarter of an hour before you noticed the light. No, we have to admit the two basic facts of the problem: Proto was at his post and the fellow entered anyway.'

'But then…,' exclaimed the superintendent, stopping suddenly.

M. Allou took him by the arm.

'I know what you're thinking. You mustn't accuse too quickly, Sallent.'

'*Monsieur le juge*, because you're here, I'm going to let you do the thinking. When there's a riddle, you're in your element. I see things more simply, but then I'm just a workhorse.'

***

They reached the car. Clermon was asleep in the back. He woke with a start when someone opened the door, and instinctively put his hand in his pocket and started to pull out a revolver.

Then he recognised his companions.

'Ah, it's you!' he said. 'But it's still night time... did you find him? I advised you not to come back if....'

'Relax,' replied Sallent. 'He's not with us.'

'Did you abandon the surveillance?'

'No, he escaped.'

'Oh!' murmured Clermon.

The superintendent recognised the implied criticism in the single syllable.

'Yes,' he said, 'we were three against one. But things happened in such a mysterious way....'

And, out of self-respect, he gave a full account of the events.

'That's certainly strange,' said Clermon at last.

Sallent had the strong impression that their companion didn't place much faith in their account and suspected they had blundered. He frowned, sat in a corner and didn't say another word.

Clermon sat down behind the wheel.

'Personally,' he said, 'I'd have liked to have got my stolen vehicle back.'

There was a grunt from Sallent's corner and M. Allou thought he heard:

'I don't give a....'

He hastened to intervene:

'I didn't hear the sound of a car.'

'Oh, it's very quiet,' retorted Clermon. 'I assume he used it and then took an express train at one of the major stations.'

'Unfortunately, the telegraph doesn't work at night in the countryside. By the time we get back to Bordeaux it'll be too late. And as for following him, he has too much of a lead.'

'How much?'

'At least an hour and a half.'

'You waited that long?'

'Double-checking,' growled Sallent.

'Besides, to follow him,' added M. Allou, 'we would have had to know the route he would take. He had a wide choice of stations from which to take an express.'

'Description posted everywhere. Will find it front of some station. Not gallivanting around France in this banger. Get on with it. Need sleep.'

'You've been very kind to put yourself out like this,' M. Allou hastened to add. 'We're very grateful to you.'

'Grateful,' echoed the superintendent.

Upon their arrival in Bordeaux, M. Allou and Sallent went straight to bed and didn't wake up until late the following morning. By the time the superintendent descended into the lobby, he found his colleague about to leave.

'Where are you going?' he asked.

'Back to Clermon's.'

'Are you following a new lead?'

'My dear fellow, I don't just think about my profession. Have you forgotten that today's the day the engagement becomes official?'

'Completely. Other things to do. Girl doesn't interest me. Without her, would've made an arrest day before yesterday. Avoided ridiculous mess last night.'

'Come, come, one must be more understanding where love is concerned.'

'Better think than talk nonsense.'

'Think then, my dear Sallent. You've nothing else to do this morning.'

'Just stupid animal. Counted on you. Too bad! Make your request. I'll go to your marriage. Much too young for you. Make fool of yourself.'

'Thank you, my friend. I'll see you soon.'

M. Allou left.

He had made his decision. Because everything he'd tried with Clermon had come to nothing, he would try to go after Serge Madras. No action had yet been taken regarding his false allegation, and he needed to make a move before it was too late. Perhaps that would bring a halt to the proceedings.

But first M. Allou wanted to take one last step.

He asked to see the secretary and was immediately taken to his office. Madras was already up, but was wearing a bandage around his head.

Seeing him again, M. Allou had to fight back his first impression. He didn't dislike the young man and it irked him to admit it.

Thus there was a harsh tone to his voice as he declared, upon entering the room:

'I've come to congratulate you, sir. I believe your engagement is due to be announced today?'

'No, sir,' replied Madras simply.

'What do you mean? M. Clermon confirmed it yesterday.'

'He forgot to ask me.'

'And you refused? Didn't you make the request?'

'I only talked about a project. Obviously, I deeply desired the marriage, and it would have taken place had my sentiments been returned. For a while I'd believed it to be so, but I was mistaken.'

'Yet Miss Clermon hasn't turned you down?'

'She's consented despite herself. I could never accept such a situation.'

'But why did she agree?'

'I can only speak for myself.'

'Of course.'

M. Allou stayed silent for a few minutes.

'Dammit!' he exclaimed suddenly. 'You strike me as an honest man. How could you have made that accusation against your rival?'

'It was genuine. I must have been mistaken.'

'No, that's not possible. There's another answer. You knew how worthless Allevaire was, but you couldn't say so publicly. So you found that means to prevent a marriage which you correctly thought would be fatal. What did you learn and when?'

'I didn't know anything!'

'Obviously you can't say anything today, so I won't press you.'

'But I assure you....'

'Goodbye.'

M. Allou shook his hand and left.

***

122

On the stairs, he heard someone coming down behind him and turned round. Marthe Clermon stepped down next to him.

'What have you found?' she asked.

He smiled.

'Be happy, my child, the marriage won't take place.'

He'd expected cries of joy, or at least a happy expression. But, to the contrary, the big blue eyes stared at him and gradually filled with tears.

'But, miss... I don't understand.'

It was not grief in her expression, but despair. In a broken voice, Marthe declared:

'I thank you, sir... I thank you very much... you've been very kind... I'm very grateful... Very... I'm very happy....'

And then she fainted.

Chapter XVII

SALLENT'S DISCOVERY

M. Allou ate lunch alone and went back to meet Sallent.

'So?' enquired the latter.

'Nothing of importance, except the proof that I'm an idiot.'

'Why?'

'There's something I don't understand.'

'About last night?'

'Oh, that's right. I'd forgotten about that.'

'Oh!'

'No, something else... something far more mysterious.'

'What?'

'The soul of a young girl.'

'No time for rubbish,' growled Sallent.

'What have you got to do that's so important?'

'Find something to do!'

'It comes with the job.'

'Not cut out for sitting thinking in an armchair. Too many riddles for me.'

'Still bothered about yesterday?'

'Yes. Something else as well.'

'What?'

'The wallet. What was it doing in Allevaire's house?'

'You say that with a knowing air, Sallent.'

'Just that I've got an idea.'

'Tell me.'

'You'll laugh.'

'No, I promise.'

'Well, I wonder if Allevaire didn't murder Fumage. Secretary here gave him an alibi. And young girl, who suspects, is afraid and doesn't want to marry Madras any more, even though she might love him.'

'She might love him? Then why protect Allevaire? So that he won't confess to Madras's complicity if he's arrested?'

'Good Lord!'

'But Madras seems like an honest man.'

'Never trust appearances.'

'So then the business in Limonest was a set-up, done by chance the same day?'

'Set-up, yes, but maybe not how you think, and not by chance.'

'Meaning?'

'Meaning you've established the right principles for the alibis, but you've applied them wrongly.'

'Explain!' said M. Allou.

'Not yet... not ready... you'd mock me. But I might take a trip to Limonest.'

'I'm going to take one into town.'

M. Allou headed for the river and, during the whole afternoon, absent-mindedly watched the big ships as they made their way to the ocean. Sallent's idea didn't seem at all stupid and he wanted to think it through to the end. Eventually, he thought he'd worked it out.

Night was falling when he decided to return. He arrived at the hotel at well past nine o'clock.

A porter came to meet him.

'A letter for you, sir.'

It wasn't stamped.

'Who gave it to you?'

'The gentleman who was with you.'

'M. Sallent?'

'Yes, that's him.'

'He left?'

'Yes, sir, he left for the station with his suitcases, about a quarter of an hour ago. He must only just have caught his train.'

'Thank you.'

M. Allou smiled to himself.

'What's he up to?' he murmured. 'Is it just because he's in a bad mood? He could have waited for me, all the same.'

He opened the envelope and withdrew a letter and an official telegram, each as brief as the other.

The wire, from Marseille and addressed to Sallent, said:

"Epicevieille signals presence of Allevaire in Limonest. Lyon *police mobile* notified. Examining magistrate Marseille, Poitevin."

It had been expedited at eight o'clock that evening.

"Well, old Poitevin's standing in for me there," thought M. Allou.

He turned to the letter and read:

"Nine o'clock. Waited to the last minute. Regards. Sallent."

'What time is the next train for Lyon?' he asked the porter.

'Tomorrow morning at half past eight.'

'Wake me at seven.'

'Very well, sir.'

***

M. Allou fell quickly into a deep asleep, unaware of the anxiety reigning at the same time in the Levalois residence in Limonest

They were seated, as usual, symmetrically one either side of their aunt Dorothée, like two vases on a mantelpiece. Occasionally, Gertrude placed her knitting on her knees and murmured:

'So, he's back....'

'You can say it as often as you like,' retorted Hortense, 'but it won't change anything.'

Gertrude fell silent, intimidated by her sister. But she brooded about the same idea, which she dared not express out loud, for fear of bringing bad luck. She feared there might be a new break-in that night, and this time the burglar, emboldened, might come to look for them in their bedrooms.

She had already got up four times to check the bolt on the door. Five minutes after the last verification, she was already unsure.

The scruple was understandable. Because what Gertrude had never confessed was her certitude that, on the night of the theft, she had indeed bolted the door. She would have been mocked if she had. So, timidly, she had tried to erase the memory, but it refused to go away.

The obsession with danger only left her to be replaced with another, older, concern, which she expressed every night. No matter how hard she tried to contain herself, she always ended by asking, in a loud voice:

'Why did you claim to recognise Gustave that night in Marseille, my aunt, when you knew very well it wasn't him?'

Dorothée never answered Gertude directly. Instead, it was Hortense who always replied:

'Be quiet. Leave our aunt alone.'

One might have thought that Hortense intervened out of the goodness of her heart, to spare the poor old woman. She had, indeed, suffered greatly from the events; her back had become more curved

127

and she could no longer walk, even with two canes, so she had to be supported.

But it wasn't only pity that justified her niece's protection—though there was plenty of that. Hortense also calculated that it would be a bad idea to annoy someone who might become rich one day; Dorothée's brother, from whom she may very well inherit, was in rapid decline.

Gertrude, more naïve, did not share the same concern. She persisted:

'You wanted to protect his escape, Aunt Dorothée, despite what he'd done. After the theft of your silverware. Without realising that could cause you problems with the police!'

It required all of Hortense's authority to shut her sister up.

She put down her embroidery and said:

'Let's go up to bed. That's better than listening to the same thing every time.'

'To bed?' murmured Gertrude. 'Aren't you afraid?'

Hortense was indeed afraid, but she realised that, if she showed it, she could provoke a panic. She had to put on a calm front.

Nevertheless, she shot a discreet glance at the bolt as she went past, which didn't escape Gertrude's notice.

'You see....'

'Of course I verify. But that doesn't mean that I think Gustave is here.'

'Yet M. Epicevieille confirms that he saw him at two o'clock.'

'I saw him this evening. He was far from certain. He's only seen Gustave two or three times in his life.'

It was a lie: the old clerk had, in fact, been adamant. But Hortense didn't want to have to listen to her sister moaning all night.

And what she wouldn't have failed to add, had she known, was that the house was under surveillance by the *police mobile*.

In any case, nothing out of the ordinary happened that night.

The following morning, Gertrude, beginning to regain her calm, had another shock at around ten o'clock. Someone had rung the door bell and, looking out of the window, she saw a very tall, thin man.

At first, she thought it was Epicevieille. But no, the visitor appeared to be much younger. So, it must be the police!

Since May 10, she had feared such a visit. Aunt Dorothée's false

128

testimony at Aubagne couldn't fail to create a catastrophe. Hopefully they wouldn't drag her old aunt into prison!

Gertrude was in a panic. What's more, Hortense had gone out. What was she to do?

A second ring of the door bell, this time much louder, prompted her to open the door, and Superintendent Sallent came in.

It wasn't his first visit to Limonest. He'd already interviewed the postman.

'Does Madam Dorothée get a lot of mail?' he'd asked.

'Oh, no, sir. Only two letters a year, and always in the same hand.'

'And did you deliver one recently?'

'Yes, about ten days ago, around May 7 or May 8, one or two days before the theft. I put it in her letter box.'

'Very good, that's what I thought.'

Now, the superintendent was standing stiffly in front of Gertrude.

She began to tremble and stutter:

'S-Sir… s-sir….'

Sallent, noticing her discomfort, adopted a pitiless stance:

'What are you hiding from me?' he asked severely.

The frightened old maid let out her secret:

'Sir, the bolt was firmly shut.'

'When?'

'The night of the theft.'

'Why didn't you say so?'

'I was afraid I'd be made fun of… I thought at the time I may have been wrong… But now I've a clear recollection.'

'Continue to refresh your memory. Did your aunt receive a letter one or two days before the theft?'

'No, sir.'

'Are you sure?'

'Yes. The only person who ever wrote to her was Gustave, and she always made us read his letters.'

'And that day she didn't show you one?'

'No, sir, I swear it. You do believe me, don't you?'

'Willingly. That's what I suspected. She must have had her reasons. But I want to be sure. Who would have looked in the letter box?'

'Whoever happened to be there when the postman arrived.'

'Sometimes that was your aunt?'

'Oh, yes, often. She was the one with the most time on her hands.'

'Very well. I'll have to talk to her.'

'Oh, sir, you're not going to put her in prison, are you? She's so old. And she loved her nephew so much. She thought she recognised him in Aubagne.'

'Just take me to her,' replied the superintendent.

Trembling, she obeyed.

***

Dorothée was still in bed.

Sallent sat down next to her and made a sign for Gertude to leave.

'Madam,' he began, 'you've given false testimony. It wasn't your nephew who was killed in Aubagne.'

'It's true,' murmured the old woman. 'I wanted him to be thought dead because of the risk of imprisonment. Is it very serious, the lie?'

'Serious? If Allevaire wasn't the victim, he could be the murderer, madam.. That would make you an accomplice to the crime.'

He had been trying to frighten her in order to get the most out of her. But he had been almost too successful, and the old woman, already very frail, was about to lose consciousness.

'Wait,' he added, in a less severe tone. 'We might be able to forgive you if you tell us the whole truth now.'

'But I don't know anything.'

'Madam, I remain astonished that three old ladies, on one particular night, neglected to bolt the door. And I've just learnt that it wasn't forgotten on the night of the theft, after all. So who would have left the door open?'

'I'll tell you everything. But don't repeat it to my nieces.'

'Of course not.'

'Oh, sir, I loved him so much, my little boy. He was like a son to me. He wrote to me so he could visit me....'

'When was that?'

'Ten days ago. But my nieces didn't want him to come here any more. I was afraid about annoying them, so I didn't dare talk to them about it. I told him to come at night... and I went downstairs to open the door for him.'

'Well, well,' murmured Sallent.

He'd expected to hear a confession about complicity: Dorothée, in his mind, had learnt about the murder her nephew was planning to commit and, unable to stop him, had provided him with an alibi by

130

simulating a theft there in Limonest. Now, in her panic, she'd handed him enough for a charge.

She continued:

'He needed some money. I didn't have any, so I gave him my silverware.'

'No, madam,' the superintendent interrupted, 'someone took five thousand francs as well.'

'That was me. I took them to give to him.'

Sallent, still maintaining his stiff posture, was softened by this act of desperation. Nevertheless, he shook his head:

'No, madam. At the time of the theft you were here, in this room, with your two nieces. Now tell me the truth. What did he do when you let him in?'

The old woman started to cry softly, and the superintendent turned his head away. At such times, he found his profession very difficult.

'He told me...,' murmured Dorothée, 'he told me go back to my room... and leave him in peace.'

Sallent got up.

She put her trembling hands together.

'Don't go, sir, listen... you see I've been sincere, and you must take that into account... It's all my fault... If I hadn't opened ....'

'Yes, madam, yes... it's not for me to judge.'

The superintendent wanted nothing more than to terminate the painful scene. But he couldn't leave, because the tremulous voice somehow held him back.

'Sir, I brought that little boy up. Badly, as you can see. I was too weak. It's my fault, not his. I'm the one to blame. And, besides, what are we talking about? I gave him the silverware, so it wasn't a theft. And I'll pay back the five thousand francs. I'll work....'

The word was obscene, coming as it was from a feeble old woman who didn't even wipe away her tears as she was crying.

'Goodbye,' said Sallent brusquely. 'Excuse me.'

He held out his hand and she clutched it between hers.

'Sir,' she moaned. 'Don't be so pitiless... towards an old woman. Think of your own mother... she would understand, if she loved you the way I loved that child. I've only ever had him in my life... nothing else except grief. I only wanted one thing, to keep him until the end. It wasn't much to ask, for a whole life. In a year, I'll be dead... I don't want my little boy sent to Guyane. I beg you, leave

131

him with me until the end!'

Exhausted, she cried in short little sobs.

It was, for Sallent, the most difficult moment of the case. He pulled his hand away, wiped her tears away brusquely and left, growling:

'What a profession. And what do I care, in the end, about the savings of those two old women? What would they have done with them? And, because of five thousand francs, I have to destroy that poor old woman. Ah, what a job! It's nearly killed me!'

He stopped and, deflecting his anger, mused:

'If only M. Allou were here. He'd take a decision. What was he doing last night? Still mixed up in sentimental stories! He's got time to waste. Anyway, he should be here in three hours.'

Chapter XVIII

M. ALLOU'S DECISION

But M. Allou hadn't taken the first train.

He'd been awakened punctually, but had taken his time getting dressed. One question concerned him and slowed him down.

"No," he said to himself, "my solution isn't perfect."

It seemed likely that Serge Madras would only have made his false accusation for a very good reason. The young man knew about Allevaire's past and, not being able to reveal anything about it, had found a way to force him to leave.

But two points remained unclear.

First of all, the attitude of Marthe Clermon the night before.

She had seemed in despair, suddenly, when her engagement was broken off. Did she love Serge Madras after all, and was it only out of scruple, because she thought him to be complicit, that she refused to marry him? But, in that case, she didn't love Allevaire. Why did Madras try to get rid of the man, then, if he wasn't a rival?

But something else worried M. Allou as well. It was the strange coincidence that the secretary had arranged his accusation for the same night that Allevaire was committing a theft five hundred kilometres away. Chance? Perhaps, but M. Allou didn't like chance and tried to eliminate it.

Once again, the concierge knocked on the door and opened it:

'It's time, sir.'

'I'm delaying my departure,' replied M. Allou in the inarticulate voice of someone thinking about something else.

'Sir has decided not to take the boat... pardon, I mean the train?'

M. Allou, staring into space, repeated slowly:

'Decided not to take the boat....'

'I meant train, sir.'

'Decided not to take the boat...,' murmured M. Allou again, nodding his head.

The concierge looked at him anxiously, ready to call for help if things got worse. But he relaxed when the guest's madness took

133

another form and he started to smile broadly, eyes gleaming, and even offered him a banknote.

'Take this, you've earned it. Yes, perfectly... decided not to take the boat.'

The man pocketed the note and made off at high speed.

'For heaven's sake,' murmured Allou once the door was closed. 'It's so simple! What an idiot I've been!'

***

He hurried after the concierge and asked him to hail a taxi.

'To a steamship company!'

'Which one?'

'Whichever one you want. The closest.'

Five minutes later, M. Allou was in a great hall and heading towards the information office.

'Did any of your boats leave on the morning of the tenth of May?'

'Yes, sir, the Rio de Janeiro, which left for Egypt with a stopover in Spain.'

'What an incredible piece of luck! I found it right away,' he murmured.

In a louder voice he added:

'Do you have the passenger list?'

'Here. The three names marked with a cross are those passengers who booked a passage and failed to turn up at departure.'

M. Allou quickly found the name he was looking for: Allevaire.

He took a printed form out of his wallet, scribbled a few words on it, signed it and put it in his pocket.

His taxi was still waiting for him outside.

'To the Sûreté,' he commanded.

Once in the office of the chief, his stay was brief. Producing the form which he had completed earlier, he handed it over:

'A summons just received from Marseille. Execute it as quickly as possible. I have to leave.'

And before anyone had time to ask questions, he was gone.

He returned to the hotel, packed his bags, and paid the bill. On the way out, he noticed the startled face of the concierge. He smiled.

'Sir,' said the man. 'It's past midday. You've missed your train.'

'It doesn't matter, my friend. On the contrary, it's perfect. But this morning you were right. Yes! Decided not to take the boat.'

***

M. Allou sent a telegram to Sallent, care of the Limonest gendarmerie, then headed over to the Clermon residence to explain the situation.

'Allevaire has returned to Limonest,' he said. 'I believe we can arrest him tonight, if I'm there. But I stupidly missed my train. You were so helpful previously that I felt tempted to ask if you could drive me there.'

'It's a long drive... But it would give me great pleasure to catch that bandit... Very well, I'll get ready. We'll leave in five minutes and be there by eight o'clock.'

'Thank you. I'm truly grateful.'

'Not at all. I'll see you soon.'

M. Allou had only been alone in the salon for a few seconds when the door opened and Marthe Clermon came in.

'I heard,' she said, looking at him with her big eyes full of anxiety. 'Sir, I beg you, don't arrest Allevaire.'

He looked at her for a long time, as if to fix that slender silhouette and fine features, tense with anxiety, in his memory. He also may have had a tinge of sadness in his eyes.

'I'm not going to arrest him,' he said at last. 'But you, too, must promise me two things.'

'Yes,' she exclaimed confidently. 'What are they?'

'First, not to cry for a whole day. Just one day. Tomorrow, many things will have changed.'

'Many things?'

'Yes, I want you to be happy, my child. You shall be... I promise. But you have to promise me as well. We both have to do our best to make it possible, without scruple. Agreed?'

'Yes,' she murmured.

'I've understood much more than you've told me. Secondly, will you think about me a little? Inspector Dupont? Goodbye, my child.'

***

When the car stopped in front of the Limonest gendarmerie, M. Allou could already distinguish, from afar, a tall figure which detached itself from the rest.

135

'Good day to you, Sallent. Did you come to wait for me? Hasn't the arrest been made?'

'No. Not in charge any more. Sick of the whole business. Let the Lyon police handle it.'

'You give up too easily. What about your motto: The job's—.'

'It's not a job,' growled the superintendent. 'I can explain if you like.'

'Please excuse us, M. Clermon,' said the magistrate, 'but it seems I'm going to have to talk to my colleague. If you wouldn't mind waiting in the café across the street, I'll join you in a minute.'

He and Sallent stepped away, but their conversation lasted three quarters of an hour. Eventually they went over to see Clermon.

'We're going to have dinner with our colleagues from Lyon. Would you care to join us?'

'Willingly.'

They had little difficulty in finding the three inspectors in the small village. Sallent introduced M. Allou.

'One of my colleagues, Superintendent Dupont, designated by Paris to take charge of the case.'

The others saluted respectfully.

'Excuse me, chief,' said one of them, 'but I'm a little confused. Has Allevaire left? If so, why did he come?'

'In any case, he's invisible,' declared a second officer.

'So what should we do?' added the third.

'What should we do?' exclaimed M. Allou. 'Why, eat, of course. It's nine o'clock and I'm dying of hunger.'

Nobody objected and they quickly found a table at a nearby restaurant. It was a long meal. At around ten o'clock, one of the inspectors summoned the nerve to ask:

'What now?'

'Now, we're going on a little trip before we go to bed.'

'As you wish, chief.'

And, leaning towards one of his colleagues, he added:

'Good idea for Paris to delegate.'

They left and started to walk along the main street. An old peasant stopped them.

'Ah,' he said, 'I'm happy to see you. I was on my way to the gendarmerie. But I believe you're the police, aren't you?'

'Yes, indeed,' replied M. Allou. 'What can we do for you?'

136

'Are you by any chance looking for the cousin of the Misses Levalois? The one all the papers have been talking about for a week?'

'Why do you ask?'

'Because if you are, I just saw him five minutes ago.'

'Where was he?' asked one of the inspectors.

'He was coming out of M. Epicevieille's house. You know, the old lawyer. He was up to no good, I'll wager. I saw one of the shutters was broken.'

'Didn't Epicevieille call for help?'

'No. And for a very good reason. Today's Thursday and he always dines *chez* Levalois and gets home late.'

'Let's take a look, just out of curiosity,' said M. Allou.

A few minutes later they were standing in front of the house, an old farm. One of the shutters on the ground floor was indeed open, and they went in.

'Oh, nice job!' said one of the men as he turned the lights on.

The dining room, where they found themselves, was in total disarray. The sideboard had been moved out of place and the drawers were lying on the floor.

But the situation in the adjacent room was even worse. The entire contents of the wardrobe had been emptied and were strewn across the floor; the mattress had been thrown against the foot of the bed.

Suddenly, a sharp order rang out:

'Come with me!'

The inspectors, surprised by the burst of energy, turned to look at M. Allou.

'Follow me!' he continued.

'Shall I come as well?' asked Clermon.

'But of course.'

They left the house, walking timidly behind M. Allou, and not daring to ask for an explanation.

The little group traversed the village and arrived in front of the Levalois villa.

'There's a lot of shouting inside,' exclaimed one of the men.

And, through the closed shutters, the sound of raised voices could indeed be heard.

'Let's take a look,' said M. Allou. 'Don't ring the bell, that'll only cause us more work, and one should always do the least possible. The door's probably not bolted, so who'll volunteer to pick the lock quietly?'

'Me,' said Sallent.

The operation was over quickly. The three men, unable to contain their impatience any longer, rushed into the house and opened the door of the dining room. The three old women were there, as well as Epicevieille. But there was a fourth person there, whom they recognised at once: Allevaire.

They seized him and held him tightly.

'Now we've got you, my lad!' said one of them.

'And why the devil are you holding him?' asked M. Allou, who had followed them in.

'But... chief....'

'Have you got an arrest warrant?'

'Yes, of course, dated the tenth of May and signed by M. Allou, the examining magistrate in Marseille!'

'Will you show it to me?'

One of the inspectors fished it out of his wallet. M. Allou took it and calmly tore it into pieces.

'You're mad,' muttered the man.

'It's the impression I've given to everyone today. Why do you want to arrest this poor devil?'

'For the theft which took place on the night before... You know....'

'What was stolen?'

'Five thousand francs and some silverware.'

'You're imagining things,' replied M. Allou. 'Look harder. Everything's there on the table, the money and the silver. Release that man. And, because you don't want to stand there empty-handed, arrest the two sisters and Epicevieille.'

'The victims?'

'Yes. It makes a change, don't you think?'

Chapter XVII

THE JOB'S THE JOB

But Hortense was on her feet immediately.

'My sister doesn't know anything about it!' she exclaimed. 'I kept everything from her.'

It was enough to look at Gertrude's incredulous face to realise she had no idea what was happening.

'All right, not her,' ordered M. Allou. 'Just her sister and Epicevieille. You don't need to hold them. They won't run away. All we need is a moral arrest. So, gentlemen, if you're in no hurry to take your charges away, I'm available to explain some of the details.'

'Yes, we'd like that. Up until now, we've just been following orders.'

'In that case, let's all have a seat. This is likely to take some time.

'No, gentlemen, Allevaire didn't commit the theft which took place here on the night of the ninth to tenth of May, for several reasons, not the least of which being that he was in Bordeaux that night.

'I should have realised earlier that a man who religiously conserves letters from his aunt (they were found in Aubagne, on the body of Fumage) would never rob her of the souvenir she cherishes the most, and which is only of very modest value.

'The reason for my error was the "material evidence" of the fingerprint on one of the spoons. Gentlemen, let me caution you against clues! Nothing is easier to fabricate, despite their rigorous appearance. Put your trust in logic instead.

'In other words, don't follow the bad example I set at the beginning of the case. The Limonest theft seemed certain and I thought it was the alibis that were false. Luckily, I refused to accept the role of chance, which is what saved me. Otherwise, I would have sent an innocent man to Guyane.'

'He's not going?' asked Dorothée.

'No, madam, not this time, at least. And never, if he's learnt his lesson.

'Are you wondering, gentlemen, how Allevaire's fingerprints could

139

have been found on a teaspoon? Nothing could be easier.

'He came here quite often because, as I've said, he loved his aunt. But his visits didn't sit well with his cousins. They were afraid of having their good reputation besmirched in the village. It wasn't very charitable, but at least it was more excusable than another motive I suspect. They were probably also thinking of the inheritance which might be coming their aunt's way, which they would like to keep for themselves, should it happen.'

'Oh, sir,' protested Gertrude.

'Isn't it true?'

'Not as far as she's concerned,' interjected Hortense. 'She's incapable of such calculations. I must confess that I....'

'Very well. Your frankness will be taken into account. So the ignoble plan was the fruit of your thinking alone, miss: separate your aunt from her nephew by accusing him of the theft of what she held dearest, her silverware.

'During your cousin's last visit, which was, I believe, three months ago?'

'Yes.'

'During his last visit, you carefully collected one of the spoons he'd used and placed it last amongst the twelve, so that no one would use it. There were never more than four of you at table, so you never used all of the silverware.

'You were planning to simulate a burglary, but then fear set in: if Allevaire succeeded in proving his innocence and was released, his vengeance might be terrible.

'So you waited, uncertain as to whether to execute your project or abandon it.

'But suddenly there was a gift from heaven: your cousin was going to leave France. The risk of imprisonment was causing him great anxiety: one more misdemeanour and he would be deported. He would go to Spain and start a new life. He booked a passage for the tenth of May.

'And I was surprised that he didn't make his plans known to his aunt personally.'

'I was wrong,' interjected Allevaire. 'I didn't have the courage, in the few days remaining, to leave Bordeaux.'

'Because of Marthe Clermon?'

'Yes. I was hopelessly in love with her. I wanted to stay with her to the bitter end, because I might not see her again, ever.'

'So you just wrote a letter.'

'How did you know I wrote? My aunt told me just now that she never received a letter.'

'Because it was intercepted. Isn't that so, Miss Hortense?'

'But, sir....'

'Oh, don't deny it. I could speak to the postman. Madam Dorothée only gets one or two letters a year, and he would certainly remember that one and recognise the handwriting.'

'How did you guess?'

'It wasn't difficult. What followed next suggests that you found out about Allevaire's departure. Do you admit it?'

'Yes, sir. I intercepted the letter so as to learn about my cousin's plans to come here. I thought if I prevented my aunt from replying, he might get vexed and stay away.'

'I see. And that's how you found out about his imminent departure?'

'Yes, sir.'

'And you took advantage. Allevaire, away from France, wouldn't be able to defend himself from the accusation of theft, which would have a damning effect on his aunt.'

'How awful,' murmured Dorothée.

'Oh, my aunt, I thought that, once he was out of the country, he wouldn't be prosecuted because nobody would be able to find him.'

'And so,' continued M. Allou, 'circumstances made possible something you wouldn't otherwise have dared to do. The only possible time to simulate the theft was the night of the ninth to tenth. Acting any earlier, your cousin could have been arrested while he was boarding and would have defended himself. He would have been found innocent and might well have taken revenge. On the other hand, acting any later would risk failure if it were discovered that he'd left the country before the theft. But that particular night worked like a charm: he would just have had time, after breaking into your home, to drive to Bordeaux and board ship at ten o'clock in the morning. It would all seem to fit together and his departure would look like flight.

'Nonetheless, being cautious and prudent by nature, you didn't think that would be enough. You knew of the extraordinary attachment your aunt had for her nephew and her obstinate denial of

141

accusations against him. She could very well refuse to believe you and suspect you of plotting her nephew's downfall.'

'Indeed,' said Dorothée, 'I never believed, despite appearances, that Gustave had committed the theft. I couldn't explain it, because my old brain can't reason any more, but I just sensed that he would never have done that to me.'

'You're right, my aunt,' declared Allevaire under his breath.

'And yet,' continued M. Allou, 'everything was organised to fool you. Your niece Hortense wanted you to hear the break-in whilst she was next to you. That way, she would appear not to be involved.'

'But how did she do it?'

'I suspected an accomplice, none other than Epicevieille. In fact, I was planning to question him tomorrow morning, during legal hours, but Allevaire saved me the trouble.'

'Yes,' interjected the nephew. 'I'd worked it all out. I went to retrieve the spoons, in order to return them to my aunt. At the same time, I found five one-thousand franc notes, which I assumed was the money my cousins had pretended I'd stolen from them. I brought them with me to confront the impostor.'

'I have to admit,' continued M. Allou, 'that the trickery was well organised. That night, at dinner, Epicevieille pretended he'd seen Allevaire in the neighbourhood. Then, later that same night, he came back into the house. It wasn't difficult: Miss Hortense had unlocked the bolt and lent him her key. He took the silverware, making sure that two spoons were left on the floor, including the one with the fingerprint. Needless to say, he wore gloves.

'And he also took the sisters' savings. No, that's not quite accurate: he hid the money elsewhere. Unless it was a payment. Maybe you'd care to comment, M. Epicevieille?'

'Yes, it was payment. What can I say? I was living in such misery. The only time I ate was here, three times a week. I was never a lawyer and was never able to put any money aside.'

'The judge will take the extenuating circumstances into account, I feel sure. After depositing the spoons, you made as much noise as possible, until the cries told you that Madam Dorothée had heard you. And then you left, without risk, because the remoteness of the villa guaranteed no cries would be noticed.

'And that, gentlemen, is the story behind the theft. You've noted how Miss Hortense exploited Allevaire's imminent departure. But she wasn't the only one to have had the idea, which has complicated things quite a bit.

'There is, in Bordeaux—or rather was, because he's now on the way to Marseille in the company of two gendarmes—a sinister scoundrel named Etrillat, nicknamed Le Borgne. You'd have been better off, Allevaire, having nothing to do with him. With such friends, all you can expect is trouble. This time it could have been serious, much worse than you think. You could very well have been killed. I'll explain in a minute.

'So, the aforementioned Le Borgne was the member of a gang, to which a certain Fumage belonged. What treason had this fellow committed? We're bound to find out sooner or later. It doesn't matter; what's important is that he'd been condemned to die by the other gang members, and Etrillat had been chosen to perform the executions.

'And Le Borgne knew of your planned departure, Allevaire.'

'Yes, I told him about it.'

'And, which was even better for him, you'd quarrelled publicly with Fumage, even making imprudent threats. The situation was perfect to brand you as the murderer. Etrillat began by stealing a few of the papers you didn't carry around with you: letters from your aunt, bills and receipts, et cetera. He then proceeded, in Marseille, in one of the spots the gang used for their rendezvous, to carry out the execution he'd been assigned. Just like Miss Hortense, and for the same reasons, he was careful to pick the night of the ninth to tenth, the only one which was plausible and free of risk.

'Afterwards, he set the stage very simply: he took the victim's wallet and replaced it with another containing the papers he'd stolen from you.

'He could, quite logically, anticipate what would happen. The letters provided the address of the nearest relatives, who would automatically be contacted. Needless to say, they wouldn't identify the body. The police, surprised, would confirm the identity via fingerprints, and would realise that the victim couldn't be Allevaire.

'But, if he wasn't the victim, could he be the murderer? That would be a natural suspicion. And if, by chance they learnt about the planned boarding the following day, suspicion would turn to certainty. And once he was in Spain, probably under an assumed name, they wouldn't be able to find him and he wouldn't be able to defend himself.'

'Ah!' exclaimed Dorothée, 'I fell into the same trap myself. I didn't believe the tale about the stolen silverware, but I conceded there had been a crime. And so I identified the body as Gustave's so he wouldn't be suspected of the other crime. But my efforts were in vain.'

'So why, then, madam, did you tell me a completely different story this morning? Didn't you open the door to your nephew yourself on the night of the theft?' asked Sallent.

'Because, sir, it seemed as though you were accusing him of murder. In which case, it would be better for him to be accused of a simple theft. I told you all that to provide you with an alibi.'

'I had no idea.'

Then, turning to M. Allou:

'You're going to have trouble pinning the murder on Etrillat,' he observed.

'Not as much as you think. An old peasant, Father Grégoire, saw him walking past after the crime, and can readily identify him.'

(That observation was borne out later.)

'But are you really sure?' persisted the superintendent. 'It could just as well have been anyone as well as Le Borgne.'

'No, I'm certain of it because of the wallet. I'll return to that later, very soon in fact.

'Because now, gentlemen, we're going to stop discussing false accusations and examine Allevaire's real activities. You don't look well, M. Clermon. No doubt you find there are too many of us in the room and the atmosphere has become stuffy. You're right, I'll attend to it right away.

'Let Madam. Dorothée and Miss Gertrude go to their rooms, inspectors, and lock Epicevieille and his accomplice up somewhere.'

When the order had been executed, M. Allou continued:

'You see, Clermon, I've sent away all the witnesses; these gentlemen are bound by their profession not to reveal anything. Oh, don't thank me, I didn't do it for you. I don't want anyone to know of your role—I have reasons for that—and nothing will leave this room.'

'Always the same thing,' groused Sallent.

'Please don't say anything. You were worried stiff this afternoon.'

The inspectors returned.

'I believe you are aware, gentlemen, of the strange adventures

144

which befell us in Bordeaux?'

'Yes, Superintendent Sallent told us. The last one is rather strange.'

'No more than the others, you'll see.

'M. Clermon, your rapid ascent in the business world has astonished quite a few people. Without any capital, you've managed to create a large business. Even given your obvious intelligence and energy, it's still a feat I find quite remarkable.

'Something else struck me. Although there had been vague talk in Bordeaux about a possible marriage of your sister to Serge Madras, you were suddenly seized by an urgent haste to announce the formal engagement to the rich young man who serves as your collaborator. And that coincided with Allevaire's intrusion into your home, once again on the night of the ninth to tenth.

'Is it presumptuous of me to think that, up until then, someone had been supplying you with funds, and that same source was about to dry up suddenly?

'Something had therefore disappeared that night, and that something was of great importance to you. Yet you hadn't gone to the police about it. What other explanation could there be than that you were in possession of letters or documents which had allowed you to blackmail someone... and that was what Allevaire took from you? Oh, don't bother denying it, I'm sure we'll find them in his pocket.'

'Here they are,' said Allevaire. 'They're letters which he procured somehow. The victim—his name doesn't matter—charged me specially to get them back. That's why I moved to Bordeaux and became part of Clermon's inner circle.

'At first I thought he kept the letters in his safe. But his secretary had access and, such was my respect for his integrity, I couldn't believe he could be an accomplice. I eventually discovered that the only piece of furniture to which he didn't have a key was the large table in the office. There could be little doubt that the letters were there.

'I made a substitute key and broke in to the townhouse. I thought Clermon wouldn't discover the theft until late in the morning, by which time I would already be on the boat to Spain, where I was supposed to hand over my package and claim my reward. I was hoping it would allow me to start making an honest living.

'The letters were already in my pocket when Madras discovered me and shone a light in my face. I ran off.

'But would Clermon alert the police and have me arrested at the port? It seemed hardly likely, given the nature of the stolen material. Nevertheless, it was a huge risk, given my criminal record. I became afraid and—.'

'—*decided not to take the boat!*' exclaimed M. Allou.

'Why are you laughing?'

'It's nothing. Just a souvenir. That phrase, spoken by chance, suddenly gave me the key to the whole case and allowed me to eliminate the coincidences which had been perplexing me. The plan to leave the country explained all the strange events of that night.

'But, Allevaire, there was no need for you to be afraid. You hadn't committed any crime.'

'How is that possible?'

'The theft was merely the recovery by a third party of something belonging to him. You can't say the letters belonged to Clermon. They belonged to the sender and you can't reproach him for having taken them back.'

'Ah, sir, if I'd thought that was the case, I would never have led such a miserable existence during those few days. But, because I thought myself guilty, I couldn't think of denying it because Serge Madras had got such a clear view of me. The only thing in my favour was something which I didn't understand: Marthe Clermon was less sure about it being me, even though I'd passed right in front of her and she couldn't have failed to recognise me. Why that indulgence?'

Clermon, who up to that point had not said a word, suddenly stood up.

'I don't want my sister compromised,' he said. 'If she didn't denounce Allevaire—.'

'—it was because of you,' interrupted M. Allou.

'How did you know?'

'It wasn't difficult. I assume that, disturbed by the noise, you, too had gone to your door and seen Allevaire pass in front of you. Serge Madras, concentrating on the pursuit, didn't notice you. But your sister did. She noticed that you didn't intervene; on the contrary, you disappeared as quickly as possible and disavowed all knowledge of the incident afterwards.'

'How could I do otherwise? Should I have tried to stop Allevaire, who would have told Marthe and Serge everything?'

'Quite so, it was out of the question,' replied M. Allou. 'But the poor child realised that you must have had a powerful reason not to intervene. She therefore chose not to confirm Madras' account, and hoped that, by making a vague statement, she could pacify both of you. Later, when she discovered Allevaire's past, she assumed you were his accomplice. As a result, she felt that she wasn't worthy to marry the man she loved, Serge. Then, when you pushed her towards that marriage, she asked me to intervene. What reason could she give other than she didn't love the young man?

'And he, not understanding the sudden rejection, assumed it was because of the charge of slanderous accusation levelled against him. So he, in turn, withdrew into his shell. Fortunately, the damage can be repaired.

'As for you, M. Clermon, you only had three ambitions: to hasten the marriage of your sister, and the formal business association which would come with it; recover "your" letters, because you had encountered unexpected resistance from the youngsters; and prevent the arrest of Allevaire, who was in a position to reveal everything.'

'That's exactly right.'

'You thought first about buying the letters from him. You guessed, correctly, that given the accusations being brought against him, he was more likely to hide than to take flight. And the fact that he'd decided not to take the boat confirmed it.'

'That's correct.'

'You also knew about his secret domicile?'

'Yes, he had occasionally asked me to phone him at that number. I made a few enquiries and discovered the address.'

'You took him a letter asking him to meet you?'

'Yes.'

'What pretext did you give?'

'I offered him a large amount of money.'

'That's not true,' exclaimed Allevaire. 'I wouldn't have come. When I work for someone I don't betray them. I kept your letter and here it is. You pretended that your sister was very sad about my departure and wanted to see me for one last time.'

'You did that...?' asked M. Allou slowly.

Clermon lowered his eyes.

'So, naturally, I went,' continued Allevaire.

'I know, Sallent and I were watching the house, hidden behind some bushes in the square. Someone opened the door for you, and today I've just discovered it was Clermon himself.'

'Yes, he made me go up to his office, where he made me the offer. I refused, upon which he flung himself on me, in an attempt to take the letters. We fought and I ran off.'

'And we weren't able to catch you,' added M. Allou. 'For three days in a row, you managed to evade us just in time.'

'Yes, the next day it was at my secret house. How did you find out about it?'

'Two other individuals were interested in you, Allevaire. First of all Madras, who hoped you would confess and free him from the charge of slanderous accusation. And then Etrillat.'

'Le Borgne? Why?'

'Because he was afraid. He thought you would begin to suspect his role in the Aubagne murder, and that you would take revenge. He wanted the upper hand, and I'm sure he tried to ambush you several times in order to kill you. He watched your house, hoping to catch sight of you through one of the windows, but you were canny enough not to show yourself.

'What to do? Should he get into your house? The door to your flat would presumably be bolted and you could very well be waiting behind it, gun in hand.

'I'm assuming he tried to lure you out and ambush you. We saw him put an envelope in the letter box.'

'Yes, it pretended to be from a friend of mine, arranging a rendezvous, but I was suspicious.'

'In passing, Allevaire, I have to say that it's strange that you needed a secret address, and strange that Etrillat knew about it. But I don't intend to dwell on the matter. I don't want to upset my friend Sallent, who is a sentimental soul. No unnecessary zeal. Let's just leave it at that.

'So Le Borgne put a message in your letter box. But he was seen by Madras, who hastened to alert us. Unfortunately, Clermon, he happened to tell us in your presence. And you didn't want Allevaire caught with your documents in his pocket.

'The second we had left, you rushed to the phone to announce your expedition. You seem to have made your announcement a few minutes too late....'

'My sister was in the lobby. I had to wait for her to go upstairs.'

'That explains why Allevaire was almost apprehended. He fled at

148

the very moment we arrived. Madras ran after him courageously, but his prey pushed him away… rather violently.'

'It was the only way, he's stronger than I am.'

'Yes… Did you know, Allevaire, that you could have been sent to prison for that? Rest assured, Madras hasn't pressed charges, so it won't happen.

'After you fled the scene, we went up to your flat and the superintendent turned on the electricity in your room. Le Borgne, who hadn't been sure you would go to the supposed *rendezvous*, was still lurking in the waste land, watching the windows. You had usually been very careful to close the shutters before turning on the light. But it's so easy to forget. Suddenly Le Borgne saw the light come on and a silhouette appear in the window, and he fired. The bullet only missed by a whisker.

'Then my friend Sallent had one of those weird ideas to which he alone knows the secret.'

'It's not a monopoly,' grunted the superintendent. 'I can name others….'

'He went to open the window! That was when Etrillat recognised him, because he'd seen us at a terrace café.'

'Yes, Proto had hailed us by our official titles, braying like an ass!'

'Don't complain, Sallent, it may very well have saved your life. Because Le Borgne, recognising you, realised that it was a police raid and had another idea.

'Because we were hot on your trail, Allevaire, it seemed unlikely to him that he'd be able to kill you before we found you. Better to provoke your arrest, conviction and inevitable deportation to Guyane, where you would be out of the way.

'But you still needed to be convicted… Now, Etrillat knew full well that you hadn't committed the theft in Limonest, because you were in Bordeaux that night, waiting to catch the boat the next day. He feared that the charges against you might not be serious enough. Therefore, you needed to be convicted of the murder in Marseille.

'So, to have the finger point at you, he devised a stratagem. He'd kept the victim's wallet and decided to take advantage of our visit to plant it in your residence.

'He reasoned that, since the light had only just come on, that our search of the premises had just started and would take some time. He therefore entered and went upstairs with the intention of placing the

149

wallet behind the coat rack, where we would find it later.

'He was able to enter the premises without trouble because he had a key. Once again, Allevaire, it's curious that he should have a key. But I'll let that pass....

'But the superintendent had heard him. Etrillat just had time to place the wallet according to plan and could logically have expected to leave unmolested—even if his presence had been detected, it would be reasonable for us to wait until he opened the door of the bedroom before challenging him. But, once again, Sallent had another of his weird ideas and bounded towards him without bothering to check whether he was armed. I must admit that, for once, it worked.

'But, for the time being, Le Borgne's plan had also worked. We had discovered the wallet.

'I tried to gain his confidence, in order that we might follow him because, at the time, I believed him to be your accomplice, Allevaire. But I can't have done a very good job, because the next day he spotted the surveillance.

'But, instead of trying to flee, he preferred to take advantage of it. He was pretty sure he knew where you were hiding, Allevaire. You had a third residence fifty kilometres from Bordeaux. That makes quite a few for an honest man, doesn't it? Let's say it was your country house. And so Le Borgne very cleverly led the inspector who was tailing him to it, hoping to have you arrested.

'And you had indeed gone there immediately after escaping from us. Well, not quite immediately: you'd stopped by briefly at Clermon's townhouse. He was doing everything he could to facilitate your escape. At the same time he phoned you about our imminent arrival, he told you he'd placed a car at your disposal. You found the key under the garage door where you, Clermon, had left it.'

'How did you know?' exclaimed the latter.

'Quite simply: the police officers saw it. I would have guessed anyway, from your embarrassed demeanour when the superintendent questioned you over the phone the following day.'

'Yes, I lost my nerve. I hadn't decided how to reply. Should I claim there was a second key, which had been stolen? It would have been more plausible, perhaps, but I was afraid of compromising my sister.'

'In any case, you didn't succeed, because I suspected, not just that, but everything else. And, out of affection for you, she confessed to everything I wanted.

150

'And now I come to our last expedition. Thanks once again to the stupidity of Proto, who has never learnt to keep his mouth shut, you, Clermon, discovered where Allevaire was hiding. Once again, you hoped he would escape and maybe, with a bit of luck, retrieve your letters.

'So, in friendly fashion, you volunteered to drive us there. It was important, however, that Allevaire not learn about your role in his pursuit, in case he took revenge by telling your sister the source of your rapid rise in the business world. You warned us not to count on you during any potential arrest. Such a precaution presented another advantage: you didn't have to stay with us and might, therefore, find an opportunity to get back the letters on your own.

'And such an opportunity did in fact arise. Allevaire doesn't respond to the door bell. Proto is left outside to guard the back of the house whilst the superintendent and I go inside to search. We leave the front door open. We've only just reached the first floor when you sneak inside. You don't go far: you limit yourself to lifting the hook securing one of the shutters. I assume, in order for it to remain unnoticed, that you balanced it delicately on the loop of the eye?'

'That's correct.'

'On our way up, we examined all the shutters carefully to make sure they were securely closed. We checked them on the way down as well, but not with the same care, naturally enough, because we were concentrating on whether anyone was hiding in any of the rooms. We left the house and moved Proto to watch the front door, which seemed by then to be the only possible point of access. You were close enough to us to hear the order given.

'After that you left, but you returned soon thereafter.'

'Didn't you check that M. Al—that M. Dupont and I had taken refuge in the cabin?'

'Yes, I did.'

'That's what I thought.'

'I also heard you talking softly.'

'And so,' continued M. Allou, 'you went quietly into the house and started looking for the letters. You didn't realise that the brief flickers of your electric torch could be seen through the slats of the shutters. The superintendent noticed them.'

'And I,' said Clermon, 'heard you coming up the stairs.'

'You handled the situation very well. My compliments. At the

151

bottom of the stairs, you crossed paths with Allevaire.'

'I was coming in,' said the latter. 'I was coming back from the village, where I'd been looking for food... at a friend's house. I saw Clermon rushing out. Needless to say, I didn't realise he'd come to my house in the company of the police, in order to break in.

'After he left, I assumed the house was empty and went in. Suddenly I heard you coming down the stairs. I turned, but you'd already recognised me. Luckily, I was able to reach my car and drive to a train station. I knew that there were no more hiding places left for me and it was only a matter of days before I was caught. But I wanted to have a clear conscience regarding the theft of the silverware, so I came here, hiding as best I could in the countryside.'

'Let that teach you a lesson,' said M. Allou.

'That I swear!'

'But I've another question for M. Clermon before he goes,' interjected Sallent. 'When we went back into the house after you'd left, we found all the shutters securely locked.'

'Of course. I shut the one I used immediately after I entered, so as to be sure not to forget. Otherwise, in a subsequent examination, you might have spotted my trick.'

'I understand. But then how were you planning to get out?'

'Through the door, whilst you were taking Allevaire away, following his arrest. I would have met you back at the car.'

'So you expected us to arrest him?'

'I couldn't prevent it. How would I see him in the dark to warn him? I took the risk that he didn't have the letters on him, and I lost. They were in his pocket.'

'You see, Sallent,' concluded M. Allou, smiling, 'he hadn't bought Proto.'

'What imbecile would waste his money on that useless creature?'

'Come now, Sallent, a little indulgence, if you please.'

'No. Always have to keep shaking him. Don't like that. The job's the job.'

THE END

APPENDIX 1

THE FRENCH LEGAL/POLICE SYSTEM

In the British and American systems, the police and prosecution gather information likely to convict the suspect. The defence gathers information likely to acquit the defendant. Arguments between the two, and the examination of witnesses, are conducted in open court, and refereed by a judge. The winner is decided, in most important cases, by a jury of ordinary citizens.

In the French system, also adopted in many other continental countries, all criminal cases are investigated by an examining magistrate. He or she is a jurist independent of the government and the prosecution service, and is given total authority over a case: from investigating crime scenes; to questioning witnesses; to ordering the arrest of suspects; to preparing the prosecution's case, if any. Much of the "trial" of the evidence goes on in secret during the investigation (confrontations between witnesses; recreations of the crime) working with the police. The final report of the investigating magistrate is supposed to contain all the evidence favourable to both defence and prosecution.

Investigations are frequently long—two years is normal in straightforward cases—but trials are mostly short. Witnesses are called and the evidence is rehearsed in court, but lengthy cross-examination in the British/American style is rare. In the *Cours d'Assises,* which hear serious criminal cases, there are nine jurors, who sit with three professional judges: other criminal cases and appeals are heard by panels of judges alone.

In France, as in Britain, the defendant is theoretically innocent until proven guilty. But in practice there is a strong presumption of guilt if an examining magistrate, having weighed the evidence from both sides over a period of several years, sends a party to court. There is no right of *habeas corpus* in France. Examining magistrates have a right (within limits) to imprison suspects for lengthy periods without trial.

Much of the leg-work during an investigation is done by the police (in towns) or *gendarmerie* (in rural areas), but relations between magistrates and police are not always as good as depicted here. Not only did anyone below the equivalent of Chief Inspector have to defer to the examining magistrate but in the 1930's they also had to cope with the Brigade Mobile—the equivalent of Scotland Yard's Flying Squad, but on a national scale—which could swoop down and usurp their powers without warning. Not surprisingly, their morale was terrible.

There are other differences between police and *gendarmes*. The police (called *Police Nationale* since 1966; before that it was known as the *Surete)* are under the control of the Ministry of the Interior and are considered to be a civilian force. The *Gendarmerie Nationale* is under the control of the Ministry of Defence since Napoleonic days and is considered to be a military force. In addition to policing smaller towns and rural areas, it guards military installations, airports and shipping ports.

Under French law, you cannot disinherit certain heirs *(les parts reserves),* as you can under Anglo-Saxon law.

APPENDIX 2

VINDRY ON THE DETECTIVE NOVEL

1. 'Le Roman Policier.' Article in Marianne, 26 July 1933

There is much talk at the moment about the detective novel; a little too much. Some praise it to the skies: and when they let go it will crash. Others relegate it to the basement: it will become covered with mould and quickly rot.

Can't we allocate it its just place? Not too high, so as not to make promises it is unable to keep, and avoid disappointment. Not too low, so as to avoid a sense of unremitting decline and the abandonment of all quality.

But in order to be fair about it, we have to recognise what it is. So many judgments have been made about it that, in reality, have nothing to do with it.

The "Detective Novel"! Under this perhaps badly-chosen heading have been lumped totally disparate works; works not without merit, certainly, but not destined for the same public and therefore sowing fateful confusion.

As with the Christmas cracker, everyone was hoping for something else and curses their luck.

Under this heading, adventure novels have been published and called detective novels on the pretext they feature criminals.

The adventure novel is about chance, the unpredictable, fantasy science and the last-minute revelation which upsets all calculations.

The detective novel is rigour, logic, real science and a solution relentlessly deduced from the given facts.

Two genres more different it is impossible to imagine.

The adventure novel is a treasure in a labyrinth; one finds it by chance after a thousand surprising detours. The detective novel is a treasure in a strong-box; one opens the door very simply with a tiny, necessary and sufficient key.

The former must present the complexity of a panorama; the other that of an architectural drawing.

The detective novel must be constructed like a mathematical

problem; at a certain point, which is emphasised, all the clues have been provided fairly; and the rigorous solution will become evident to the astute reader.

No, the presence of a criminal is not enough to turn an adventure novel into a detective novel.

Conan Doyle and Gaston Leroux, in several works, were the masters of the detective novel; Wallace, that of the adventure novel.

Something else as well, delivered under the same heading: the police novel.

It includes shoot-outs, rooftop chases, opium dens, made-up detectives and cries of horror.

The detective novel, on the contrary, economises on revolvers and the police chases of pre-war films.

It lets you into the dining-room, with the meal already prepared, and not into the kitchens.

It is not a work of realism or a documentary; it is constructed for the mind. The logic is unreal, or rather, surreal. The master of fact and not its slave.

One cannot accuse it of an "unhealthy influence on youth," for it interests only the intelligence.

So we have three essentially distinct genres:

The adventure novel, about the life of the criminal.

The police novel, about the arrest of the criminal.

The detective novel, about the discovery of the criminal.

And even, dare I say, "discovery" pure and simple: for the criminal and the police are mere accessory elements to the detective novel. Its essence is a mysterious fact which has to be explained naturally; the criminal hides his activities and the detective tries to discover them; their conflicts provide convenient situations: the "givens" of the problem. That's it.

True detective novels are only "police novels" by accident. Maybe we should change the name.

I propose: "Puzzle novel." (1)

Does this confusion between the detective novel, the adventure novel and the police novel result solely from a badly-chosen term?

No: all three possess a common element of fascinating importance: action. Overwhelmed by the speed, one no longer notices the body moving.

(1) *Roman probleme:* "problem novel," or "puzzle novel" (less confusing).

Action dazzles the reader. Alas, it sometimes dazzles the author: of what use is style if the intrigue is enough to excite passion? Superfluous dressing which can only slow down the chase.

Style, however, is not a gilded ornament to be taken out of the wardrobe on festive occasions; it must be true to itself to the end. An umbrella has its own style if it remains perfectly umbrella.

The detective novel has a right to its own style, just like everything else. It can demand its own language, for it stutters in the others.

Its phrasing must be unadorned, the better to fly with the action.

Its narrative must contain everything necessary, but nothing more.

The detective novel, as opposed to the psychological one, does not see the interior but only the exterior. "States of mind" are prohibited, because the culprit must remain hidden.

It's only necessary to reveal what can be seen *immediately* in the action; but to do it properly, by which I mean rigorously; look for the aspect which has impressed the spectator to the crime.

"The cry of horror" is a bit vague. And generally inaccurate: gendarmes very seldom let out cries of horror; and the civil police scarcely more.

No, a detective novel isn't necessarily "badly-written."

It can, incidentally, possess other qualities; one only needs to read the marvellous "atmospheres" of Simenon, who has imposed his intensely personal touch on the genre.

But I've only tried here to bring out the salient aspects of the detective novel or, if you will allow me, the "puzzle novel":

An action;

An equation;

A style.

Perhaps it will then be easier to assign it its proper place.

No, it's not very high: it doesn't lift the spirit in any way; it's a sort of crossword: a simple game of intelligence.

No, it's not very low; it seeks to tap into our need for logic and our faculties of deduction. There's nothing shameful about that.

It's an honest and respectable genre: nothing grandiose and nothing unhealthy. One can, without shame, experience pleasure or boredom equally well. But it's ridiculous to venerate it or despise it.

It can be the source of works that are bad, mediocre or good: and even brilliant if they are signed by Edgar Poe—but they contain a "special something," it's true; even so it's important to acknowledge that Edgar Poe used this mould in which to pour his "precious metal."

157

2. Extract from a 1941 Radio Francaise broadcast

"Why did I give up the detective novel? For no particular reason: the way one gives up a game one no longer finds amusing. Because the detective novel is nothing more than a game; nothing more and nothing less. Like chess and crossword-puzzles, it has its rules, which constitute its honesty and dignity. I tried my best to play by them and was only interested in the logic: in the problem properly posed and correctly answered."

"In the puzzle?"

"Yes, in the puzzle. Much more so than in the drama or the adventure. I wanted to excite the reader's intellect more than his passion. I don't regret in any way having written detective novels. It was a game where I didn't cheat. If I stopped writing them it's because the game had ceased to amuse me, and one shouldn't write when one doesn't feel like it."

"Can you identify the reason for this change of heart? Or does it remain obscure, even to you?"

"I think I understand. It's gruelling work, but with moments of sheer pleasure and more fascinating than any other game. But now that I'm writing real novels—."

"Les Canjuers, La Cordee, and last year La Haute Neige?"

"Yes, since then I no longer play with my characters, I collaborate with them and I live with them. It's a solemn joy, far from amusement."

3. Extract from Letter to Maurice Renault, editor of "Mystere- Magazine" October 26, 1952

What's the oldest French detective novel? I believe it's Voltaire's "Zadig." A short novel, but rather too long to be a short story.

It conforms to what I believe to be the definition of the genre: "A mystery drama emphasizing logic."

So, three elements:
1. A drama, the part with the action
2. A mystery, the poetic part
3. The logic, the intelligent part

They are terribly difficult to keep in equilibrium. If drama dominates we fall into melodrama or worse, as everyone knows; if

158

mystery dominates, we finish up with a fairy tale, something altogether different which doesn't obey the same laws of credibility; if logic dominates the work degenerates into a game, a chess problem or a crossword and it's no longer a novel.

A great example of equilibrium? "The Mystery of the Yellow Room."

CPSIA information can be obtained
at www.ICGtesting.com
Printed in the USA
LVHW01s0156020518
575656LV00010B/235/P